THE
CLIENT

KAT GOSS

Hylosis Publishing LLC
hylosis.pub

Copyright © 2025 by Kat Goss
All rights reserved.

ISBN eBook: 979-8-89403-016-6
ISBN Paperback: 979-8-89403-017-3
ISBN Hardcover: 979-8-89403-018-0

To my Ouma
who taught me that
even the most ordinary days
can hold the most captivating stories

TABLE OF CONTENTS

THE CLIENT

CHAPTER ONE

WITH EACH ICY DROP that landed on her skin, Natalie's already miserable mood worsened. She tugged on the leash, but Barley wouldn't give in. Of all the cattle dogs she'd ever owned, he was by far the most stubborn.

A strand of messy, walnut hair clung to her cheek as she blinked the rain out of her eyes.

"Come on, Barley," she urged, tugging on the leash, but Barley only stared at her with blank eyes. He'd been difficult since they moved. He was accustomed to larger rooms and quieter days. Their new home was a small cottage outside the city with a tiny garden that was entirely overgrown and chaotic.

Some days it felt as if there was no room to breathe at all—precisely what had prompted their walk in the first place.

Still, the breeze picked up and stung her skin through her clothes. She was too tired to remain patient.

Soaked through her clothes, Natalie reached into the car and pulled Barley into her arms and under the downpour with her. It was tough to lift him with only her small frame to keep him up.

"Your breed is meant for the farmlands, have you forgotten?" she said to Barley. "Now come on. I want to shower and get warm."

Barley dragged his feet as they struggled toward the front door. The dog wasn't the only one reluctant to step into the home. Natalie and David had been fighting all afternoon. Since she'd taken the time to go on a hike with Barley, she had no idea what she was walking into.

"We can't wait out here forever," Natalie whispered and pushed the door open.

Inside, the house was dead quiet—a rare occasion. David, a film editor, usually had some form of repeating sound snippet coming from his office accompanied by frustrated mumbling. Things were only ever that quiet when he had his headphones on. And he only ever had his headphones on when he was in a particularly foul mood.

The small, beige home felt heavy with their moods. While it was like that often, it thankfully wasn't ever like that for long.

Natalie padded down the hall to take a shower, hoping it might put her in better spirits. Then, there might be a chance her and David would be speaking to each other again by the time dinner came around.

The warm flow of the water replaced the cold wet of her skin, letting it rush over her head and face. Her fingers and toes were so cold that the steaming water burned for a moment as she acclimatized.

It wasn't surprising that she and David fought often. Their young marriage had been put to the test within the first few months of living together. As with many marriages, the tension was rooted in their finances.

Natalie stayed in the shower until it started to cool. When she shut off the tap and stepped out of the bathroom, she felt all was well again.

The bed creaked beneath her as she sat to rest her feet. Her eyes closed and she basked in the silence. Except for the sound of the rain, she could hear little of the world around her.

The smell of food wafted in from the kitchen. In their small home, it took only a few steps to find her way there.

Natalie strolled into the kitchen and sat down at what used to be the dining table. Their new house had no dining room. It consisted of two bedrooms—one of which had become David's office—a small kitchen, an even smaller bathroom, and a living room that doubled as Natalie's workspace.

"It smells *divine*," she said, testing the waters.

"I want to make it up to you," David said with a kind smile that reached his eyes. "I feel bad."

His hair was a mess—the way it often was when he'd been scratching at it, dealing with a difficult thought. He had replaced his t-shirt from earlier with another one that seemed to have been dug out from the back of their shared closet. It was creased and worn, but it was one of her favorites.

Natalie shook her head. "Don't feel bad," she said. "This is my fault. All of it."

David slid a glass of red wine over to her. She gladly accepted it, eager to call an end to a particularly tough day.

"You're not the one who spent the money," he teased.

"It's your money. You should be able to spend it how you like. You don't need me jumping down your throat over every penny. I'm just stressed," Natalie explained.

"We're married. It's *our* money. And you're right, we don't have the pennies to spend."

Natalie filled her mouth with wine, not letting it linger on her tongue for even a moment before swallowing it down. That was one thing she loved about David. Even though their fighting had become more frequent, it was never drawn out.

"It's my fault we're in this position," Natalie confessed. "I should never have relied on a single client. It was foolish."

David reached over and put a kind hand on hers. "You couldn't have known what would happen. I mean, you worked with him for years. I can understand why you trusted him. What you went through would be tough for anybody to cope with."

In one day, she had lost her only client—and along with him, the ability to pay her own bills.

"I just don't understand," she said softly. "For three years I edit his work. No matter how late or how tight the deadline was. Then suddenly, he's silent. I never hear from him again. No explanation, no new work, nothing."

David came around the table and put his arms around her. She wished desperately to find the comfort she needed in his embrace, but it would take a lot more than a good hug to sort through their problems. The loss of work and income had cost them almost everything. They'd had to sell their home and rent a smaller one. It had been the only way to get out of debt.

"I just, I see how hard you work to make ends meet for us," Natalie's eyes welled up. "How was I to know he never published any of the work he sent me? I have *nothing* to show for it—no official portfolio. All this time I assumed I was creating a name for myself as an editor. I feel foolish."

"You're trying to get work. You're searching for new clients every day," David said gently. "I can see the effort. Please, don't be so hard on yourself."

"This is not how I wanted things to go," she said, holding back her tears. "We were supposed to be happy and carefree newlyweds. Now, we're just putting out a new fire every day."

"Speaking of fire…" David rushed over to pull the pan off the stove.

He wasn't the best cook, but he loved to do it, and Natalie loved any meal she didn't have to cook herself. She refilled her glass as he plated their pasta.

"Barley was soaked when I saw him earlier," David said, gracefully changing the subject.

"We got rained on. He refused to get out of the car, and I had to carry him."

David's eyes widened. "I'm glad to hear I'm not the only one who struggles with him. Also, that I'm not the only one who's in the dog box today."

"He likes you," she said with a laugh. "He just likes me more. And you're not in the dog box. We were just having a difficult conversation."

In truth, Barley didn't care much for David. He would wedge his way between them when they sat beside each other and sometimes even while they slept. It was cute, but it was also one cause of their arguments.

"I hate this," she whispered.

"It's not so bad," he comforted her. "We have a roof over our heads. We have Barley, and this delicious plate of pasta."

"Don't pretend this doesn't suck," she argued. "This isn't what you signed up for when you married me. I feel responsible."

"Hey." He placed a finger beneath her chin and tilted her head to face him. "I signed up for a life with you. That's what I have now. Nothing is perfect, but I'm happier than I've ever been. Days like today, I fear I'll lose you. I don't think I'll ever face a greater fear."

She tried to smile, but it felt strained. She felt as if she might not ever stand proudly on her own two feet again. She'd always hated the notion of relying on a man for survival. Perhaps she needed to deal with her own ego.

Her meal was pleasant enough. They laughed and chatted about insignificant things as if they hadn't been screaming at each other hours before.

"How was work today?" she asked, returning the subject to something more real.

"It was alright," he answered. "Although I must admit, phone ads are my least favorite. They never make any sense to me."

"Well, how do you sell something that everybody already has?"

He smiled. "There you go again, editor of anything and everything. I mean, the ads work, I guess. Why else would they keep making them?"

Their careers had been so similar and so different at the same time. David was a film editor, while Natalie was a line editor. Both of them had been working as freelancers when they met. That was technically still the case, but Natalie had close to zero client work left. Every few days she got a blog post to proofread, but that was it.

"I'm not an editor," she said. "Not anymore. Not unless I'm actually editing anything."

David clenched his jaw, and she knew better than to continue with that train of thought. It would only lead to further arguments. They had enough of that for the day.

Barley came to curl up at her feet as her glass was filled a third time.

"You'll get back to it," he said. "I know you will. You're fantastic at what you do."

She gave him a weak smile. "It's difficult after Alan. It's hard to explain and it must make me look so silly."

"Relying on one client for your confidence?" he asked. "It's a little silly, but who am I to judge?"

Alan had kept her career afloat. He had given her every and any editing work he required. Each year, he paid her more. She had become accustomed to the lifestyle provided by him, while never truly knowing him.

Then as suddenly as he'd appeared, he'd vanished again. She had submitted work to him one morning and never heard from him again. While someone else might have assumed he'd simply gotten carried away with other pursuits, Natalie assumed it was because she'd done an outright horrendous job of editing his work. Then, when she began putting a portfolio together to approach other clients, she learned none of her work had ever been released to the public.

It was a career knock she feared she would never recover from. In the end, she had fallen so far behind on her mortgage payments that they were forced to sell the house. Her new marriage was meant to be *growth*—exciting and fruitful. Instead, she felt an immense guilt she wasn't sure would ever dissipate.

That night, as David slept deeply beside her, Natalie lay awake, wondering how she might ever come back to her old self. All her life, she had wondered how women could be duped into sending money to internet lovers or traveling to meet strangers they believed they were in love with. Now, she herself had built a sort of relationship with a man she had never met and had no intention of being romantically involved with—yet she still checked for news from him every day.

It was enough to keep her staring at the ceiling while the rest of the world slept. And in the day, it occupied her mind, souring her thoughts and dirtying her mood until it drove a wedge between her and the only man she'd ever *actually* fallen in love with.

She felt like the world's biggest fool.

CHAPTER TWO

DAVID'S SCHEDULE HAD HIM working all day, tucked away in his office where nobody was allowed to enter. Natalie only ever saw it a handful of times when she'd delivered a coffee or some lunch. Despite the anxiety-inducing cleanliness of the room, the kind of work he did had a way of irritating even the most patient of people. He would slide back and forth on scenes, each time playing the same one-second-long snippet of sound. It would drive the sanest of mind straight to madness.

Natalie, on the other hand, preferred to work after the sun had set. That way, she had plenty to keep her mind busy instead of staring at her bedroom ceiling in the silence of each night. Most nights, she and David were at their desks instead of in each other's company.

She didn't really have much work to do this night, and that was a problem. So, she had convinced herself that it was a good time to work on her book. A story of a woman who had fallen through the

Earth's crust and into the depths of Hell, where she'd fallen in love with the devil himself. She wasn't entirely convinced of the plot, or the idea, or her capabilities, but it was a welcome distraction.

She had all of three hundred words written before she got stuck.

Her mind was so full of thoughts that nothing could be heard over the din. Frustrated, she pushed back her chair, rattling her desk in the process. She walked softly over to David's office and raised her hand, ready to knock.

The thought of disturbing him scared her. It pounded through her chest and suddenly she realized that she would not know what to say if he answered the door. One argument had been enough for that day.

She should be thanking him by letting him focus. Not disrupting him.

Her hand lowered, and feeling defeated, she returned to her desk. There was a sadness that crept in, nestling among all the other angst she already had brewing within her. She slumped back into her chair.

The page stared back at her like her greatest enemy. She would tap a few words on her keyboard and promptly delete them over and over again. All it was really good for was destroying her confidence further and making her feel as though she was slowly losing her marbles.

Natalie rubbed her eyes so many times that the hairs of her eyebrows were brushed in all the wrong directions. The last three sips of her coffee were ice-cold at the bottom of her mug.

Despite the weeks she'd spent perfecting the outline, she had never truly considered who the devil would be. In her mind, she modeled him after Alan, thinking it would help her move on. The only problem being that she didn't actually know anything about him. While his travel stories were incredibly heartfelt and sweet, they didn't tell her much more about him.

She had no idea how to describe the devil. Horns seemed cheesy, but so did anything else she considered. She couldn't exactly settle for a featureless void, either. That was nothing to fall in love with. For a short while she considered making him a ghostly figure in the night, but that was hardly something she could convince was lovely.

Natalie stared at her screen as she tapped her fingers against the edge of her desk. It was already almost midnight, and her mind wasn't ready for sleep.

She perked herself up. "You're a professional," she reminded herself out loud.

Her fingers hovered over the keys, still as ever. Not a single word came to mind. Instead, she tried to force it.

His eyes were dark like morning coffee.

Delete.

Nothing in the space around her made sense until he smiled.

Delete.

She had expected a red creature, a demon so frightful it would terrify her away from him. Instead, she saw such a complex beauty dressed in scars that she wanted to reach out and hold him. She wanted to make things right.

Delete.

"This is useless," she whispered. "What are you thinking?" Evidently, she wasn't thinking at all.

Who was she to write romance? She'd hardly known it in her life at all. David had been the first person she'd ever loved. The only man she couldn't live without.

Before him, men had bored her. Not that she was a particularly interesting person, but they had been unable to offer her what she could already offer herself. Natalie had always paid her own bills and found her own peace. She had Barley for company. It always seemed to her that men had little to offer.

Once David came into her life, it immediately felt as if he already knew her. He knew just what to say, and how to behave.

```
He looked at her as if he knew her, as if her presence
there was nothing new to him. She wanted to speak,
but perhaps he already knew what she would say. She
was afraid in a way that excited her…
```

Delete.

Natalie collapsed into her folded arms and groaned. She'd spent years working in publishing and couldn't come up with one decent description for her protagonist.

She highlighted the few hundred words she had and deleted them all, faced again by a blank page. Somehow, it was comforting— familiar. And she wasn't in a hurry, anyway.

Natalie had no deadlines looming. The book was more of a way to show David she was working on something. However, a blank page felt she was failing him.

After all those hours of work, she had nothing to show.

"What are you doing?" she asked herself quietly.

It was simple. She could fix her portfolio and send out some emails. Eventually, she would get some decent work. Why then did it scare her so much? Every time she opened the folder labeled "portfolio" she felt sick to her stomach.

She thought about Alan. Why did she miss him so much when he was nothing but a stranger to her?

The answer was simple. With the amount of work he'd given her, Alan's writings occupied all her days. Every morning when she woke up, she read a piece of him that he'd typed out the night before. Day after day, she peered inside his mind.

The way he wrote seemed so personal. As if he had written down a secret and she was the first one to know it. Despite his writing never being particularly *good*, she had often waited to see what the next installment would hold.

Natalie hovered her mouse over the last piece of writing he had sent her and double-clicked.

```
How could the world know just how far I would reach
to pluck you from its branches? How desperate I am to
know your touch? Even the tears that roll from your
cheek bless the Earth, watering the ground so that
life may blossom in your wake. There is no greater
beauty than the mystery of you.
```

It was different to his other work. He'd always written travel books, but had wanted to attempt something more emotional. She enjoyed the change before it came to an abrupt end.

That was how far she read before she closed the document. Natalie had never once asked who he wrote about. At first, she assumed he was merely writing romantic fiction, but eventually it became clear he had a muse. She had never even asked him what the passages were for. Her job was just to edit and send it back to him. That was all.

"Good night," David mumbled as he headed past her toward the bedroom.

"See you later," she responded without so much as looking in his direction.

It was no use. She would get no writing done that night and what difference was there between staring at her bedroom ceiling and her computer screen? At least when she lay in bed, she was more comfortable.

She checked her email one last time before heading to bed. She expected the usual spam messages. Checking her email was her one last attempt at hope each night. Sometimes, there would be another blog post to edit. Those were alright; they paid a few bills.

What she really hoped to see was Alan's name, followed by an explanation and an apology.

That night, she saw Alan's name. But there was no apology.

```
From: Amanda Peckin
Subject: Alan Peckin - Any information?
```

Natalie's hand trembled as she clicked on the message. She blinked to clear her tired eyes of blurred vision and fight back her nerves.

```
Dear Natalie,

My name is Amanda Peckin, and I am Alan's wife.
```

I have been investigating his disappearance. The police have been of no help, I'm afraid, so I've turned to a private investigator. We've found you are the last person he contacted. The police believe he has left me, but I believe something else has happened to him.

I must ask if you've heard from him recently? Perhaps from another mailing address or in a different format? Do you know where he is?

We'd like to speak with you. Please help me if you can.

Desperately,
Amanda

Natalie's mouth dried.

The email had found her far from well, and it only made things worse. But finally, she had an explanation. Something she'd always wanted.

Alan was an actual missing person. He had disappeared not only on her, but the rest of the world, too.

She didn't know what to do or think.

She chewed at her nails as she read the email over and over again, as if she might read something different with each pass through. At least she learned one thing about him: he had a wife.

Why would Amanda think she knew where he was?

There were so many questions in Natalie's mind that it felt as if a hot spike had been pressed into her temple, through her skull and was slowly making its way to the center of her brain.

Barley stretched out on the sofa and let out a soft, tired groan. Natalie rubbed her eyes; they were beginning to grow sore from being so tired. She took a deep breath and let it out slowly.

She got up and stretched before walking quietly over to Barley. Natalie kissed him on the head.

"Come on then," she whispered. "Let's go to bed."

Barley blinked a few times, stretching his own legs before hopping off the sofa and following her to the bedroom a few steps away. There, she felt her way through the dark until she found her side of the bed.

Natalie pulled her sweater off and wormed her way beneath the covers. She tried as hard as she could not to wake David, but when Barley hopped up to lie across her feet, he stirred.

"Sorry," she whispered, as she did every night.

David squinted at the clock beside his bed. "You're in bed early," he said. "Did you have an inspired night?"

"Not exactly," she answered. "I deleted it all."

David turned to face her and tucked his arm beneath his pillow. The covers masked his yawn as he blinked a few times. "Deleted? Why?"

Natalie sighed. "I know it's odd, but I just hated it. It just didn't feel real. I'm an editor, and I would never have let that kind of writing be published."

"Well, we are our own worst critics," he said.

He was being supportive, but she heard the hint of disappointment in his voice.

Her mind was bursting with a million thoughts, and she knew that if she did not voice them then, no matter how tired her husband was, that they would keep her from her sleep all night.

"There's something important," Natalie said.

"Oh?"

"I got an email from Alan's wife," she explained, and David immediately perked up. "He's missing. Vanished. She and her private investigator want to speak with me."

CHAPTER THREE

DAVID SAT UP IN bed and turned on his bedside lamp. "Missing?"

Natalie nodded. "It certainly explains a lot. All this time I thought it was something I did. That he simply never had the heart to tell me I was doing a terrible job."

David took her hand squeezed it tight. "You're an excellent editor."

"I've gone years without any concrete proof of that," she said. "Alan sent me work, sure, but he never praised me for any of it. The need for that never crossed my mind until he was gone."

"What did his wife say, exactly?"

Natalie took a deep breath. She pulled the covers up so that they tucked away more of her, sheltering her from both the cold air and her insecurities.

"I'm the last person he spoke to," she said. "Well, he sent me work. I guess that's why the private investigator wants to speak with me."

"Does that mean anything? Private investigator? This sounds serious."

She shrugged. "I don't know. I mean, Amanda wants to know if he's been in contact with me since. I don't know what to think of that."

David stared ahead. She had not expected him to take the news quite that badly. He seemed lost in his thoughts, consumed by the information as if it was a breaking news headline.

"I'm sorry," she said. "I've woken you from sleep and this is a lot to take in."

"No," he said quickly. "I'm glad you've told me. This is important."

David seemed far away. Natalie didn't know how to feel. Was she supposed to be pleased that it was no fault of her own that Alan had stopped contacting her? Did she need to feel concerned? Was it reasonable to worry that she might be part of the investigation into a missing person?

"I suppose he won't miraculously come back with more work, then," Natalie said. "I could dream, couldn't I?"

"You'll write your book," David said. "I'm sure it will be great. Then I can proudly say that I am married to a famous author."

"My book," Natalie scoffed. "I've been at my computer for three hours now and I left there with less words than when I sat down. That's literally the opposite of writing a book."

David chuckled. "True. But only because you don't settle for anything less than perfection."

"This book could take me a long time. I'm not sure we can afford that," Natalie said. "I keep trying to get myself together and find work, but I've just hit a wall. I must seem so pathetic to you."

"We've spoken about this," David responded. "It's not pathetic. Besides, we still have a roof over our heads."

"What will we do one day when we don't?" she asked. "What if I never make it out of this hole?"

"That won't happen," he said kindly. "Besides, if all we have is a cardboard box to separate us from the outside world, I'll be happy as long as I share it with you."

She nestled into him, and he wrapped his arm around her. Her world was small. It consisted entirely of David and Barley. By the time David met her, she had no family left. Her parents had both already passed away, and Natalie had been an only child.

Natalie had always been so desperate for attention, yet simultaneously suspicious of it. Luckily for her, David had been charming enough to break her paranoia and ease her desperation in one perfect swoop.

"You're stressing too much," he said.

"I think I'm stressing just the right amount," she answered. "*You're* working so much that I hardly see you. How long before you burn out?"

"You'll get work before then," he urged. "You just need a little more time to find your footing. You know, I've been thinking… Perhaps the reason you're having a hard time finding your confidence is because deep down, you don't want to be an editor anymore."

"Don't be insane," she said. "That's all I know. If I'm not an editor, what else will I do?"

"Well, when you finish your book, you'll be an author," he answered. "And there are many things to do in the world. You're bound to find something else you like eventually."

"I hope so," she said.

Natalie was tired of having the same conversations with David, but there was nothing else happening in her life. She had nothing else to talk about. She felt bad that he was stuck with such a boring wife.

Although, he would argue with her on that point.

"I'll try again tomorrow," she said meagerly.

"I know you will."

Natalie lay on her side, and he joined her, his arms over her as she snuggled into him. Barley sighed at her feet as she tucked her toes beneath his warmth.

"I'm sorry to hear about Alan," David said. "It must be quite a shock."

"I just don't know what to think," Natalie said. "And I don't know what his wife wants from me, either."

"She just wants to know what happened to her husband," David said. "She's going to ask anybody she can. Wouldn't you do the same if I ever went missing?"

Natalie couldn't even begin to fathom it. She had become so accustomed to having David around that a world without him seemed impossible to navigate.

"I'd be lost," she said.

"In that case, if I ever decide to pull a disappearing act, I'll remember to take you with me," he teased.

Natalie chuckled. "Deal."

While the warmth of her bed and her husband made her feel safer from the world, it was no comfort for her mind.

"He was a large part of your life," David said. "It's normal for you to feel grief."

"I didn't really know him, though," Natalie said. "At most, we would leave witty comments somewhere on the side of the document. I have no reason to grieve for a stranger."

"You might not have known any details about him," David explained. "But he was present in your day every day. That counts for so much more than you realize."

He was right. After all, people missed their favorite radio presenters, even though they'd never met them before. The world mourned for actors they never truly knew, and strangers who suffered in war-torn countries.

Alan had been a steady part of her day for years, until he suddenly wasn't.

"What do I say to his wife?" Natalie asked.

David sighed. "Nothing. You aren't involved and you did nothing. If I were you, I would just leave it. You would only be wasting her time without any information to offer."

"She must be desperate if she's reaching out to me," Natalie said. "I feel too bad to say nothing."

"Well, that's up to you. Just be careful. This is not something you want to be involved in. She's looking for threads to pull. If she's that desperate, she could read into anything you say. It could get ugly for no good reason."

"You're right," she said.

David snuggled up to her and she felt his breathing grow slower. He would soon be asleep again, a power she was increasingly envious of. Natalie took a deep breath and held it a moment, then she released it as slowly as she could.

She closed her eyes and tried to count backward from one hundred to zero, then back up again. Nothing worked. She could not get herself to sleep. Natalie tossed and turned and fluffed her pillow a hundred times.

"I'll make you some tea," David offered after the third time he'd woken up from her faffery.

"No, it's alright," she argued, guilt seizing her.

"It'll help," he said with a kind smile.

David kissed her on the cheek before slipping out from beneath the covers. His dark hair stood in a thousand different directions as he staggered the few steps toward the kitchen.

With each passing day, she became more grateful for him. He was the only thing which stood between her and defeat most nights. He dragged his feet back into the room, a steaming cup of chamomile tea in his hands.

"Here you go," he said softly.

He tried to smile but he was too tired. His eyes were only half open as he fell into bed and pulled the covers over him again. Natalie sat up and sipped at her tea as she watched his chest rise and fall softly until he entered a deep sleep again.

She thought of Amanda then. Did she watch Alan sleep with such fondness until one day he simply didn't return home? Was she staring at the empty half of the bed each night wondering where he'd gone?

In that sense, Amanda and Natalie had a lot in common. They both wanted to know what had happened to Alan.

Natalie could hardly remember what she did each night in bed before David came into her life. How had she managed to sleep alone for so long without the comfort of another slumbering soul at her side? Would she ever be able to cope with being alone again?

Where was Amanda when she had written the email? Had she been alone in her quiet home, thinking of Alan? Had she been sitting next to his empty spot in their bed?

She couldn't possibly say *nothing* to her.

The woman had lost her husband. She was lonely and likely worried and afraid. How could Natalie simply leave something like that unanswered? The least she could do was let Amanda know she'd reached a dead end with her and offer her sympathies.

As Natalie ran through all the different ways she might respond to Amanda, her mind eventually grew quiet enough to let her sleep.

Her dreams that night were a jumbled mess of words. The writings Alan had sent her meshed with those she had deleted from her book. A story played out in her mind of Alan and the devil. They sat together as they discussed all the intricate details of love and loss. It had been some time since Natalie had dreamed anything at all, let alone something so odd and confusing.

She did not wake until the sun was already high in the sky and David had long disappeared into his office. For a brief moment after waking to the empty space beside her, she panicked, imagining David had disappeared from her life like Alan from Amanda's.

Natalie held her ear up to his office door and listened as the same sound of a car engine started and stopped six times in a row. Knowing he was just beyond the door gave her comfort.

The steam from her coffee swirled against the cold air as she walked slowly toward her desk. Natalie sat down at her computer. Her sleepy, bed-headed face stared back at her in the black of the screen.

She went directly to her inbox to make sure the email from Amanda had not also been part of her dream. There it was, still open—along with the blank page once holding the first few hundred words of her book.

CHAPTER FOUR

NATALIE FACED THE SAME day she had faced for weeks. She needed to look for work, she hoped to get some writing done, and at some point, Barley needed to be walked. First, though, she needed to write a response to Amanda.

She clicked the reply button and stared at the blank box, waiting to be filled with words.

For someone who worked with words for a living, she certainly had a difficult time choosing her own.

Amanda,

You can't imagine how surprised I am to hear from you. I'm sorry, but I haven't heard anything from Alan for months. In fact, I've been wondering all this time what happened.

I'm sure you can understand my shock to learn that he is considered a missing person. I'm sorry I can't be of more help. I wish I could.

I'm not even entirely sure what his work was for. As far as I know, none of it was ever published.

Let me know if there's more I can do to help.

Sincerely,
Natalie

It felt silly to offer her help. There really was nothing Natalie could do. It solidified that Alan would not suddenly come back into her life and fill her pockets. Unsuspectingly, it gave her the push she needed.

For the following two hours, she worked on her portfolio. It wasn't nearly as impressive as she would have wanted it to be, but it was honest, and it would have to do. If only she could decide where to send it to.

She scrolled for what seemed like hours through lists of possible positions and new clients to approach. That was as far as she got—a scribbled list of names and email addresses in the notebook beside her computer.

Natalie wished desperately to ask David for help, but there was one very strict rule in their home. While his office door was closed, he was not to be disturbed. So, Natalie turned to a cup of coffee in the hopes of some answers. Or at the very least, an ease from her guilt.

All that time she had assumed that Alan's sudden disappearance from her work had been her fault. That she'd been so focused on her new relationship and planning the wedding that she'd dropped the ball on quality.

She wasn't sure why she was carrying it all so heavily. It wasn't her burden to carry. Why, then, was she struggling to move on from it all?

Barley nudged her legs. Natalie was the result of a life dedicated to a job. She had never bothered to develop any hobbies or even learn which kind of music she enjoyed best. All she had ever done was throw herself into her work.

David, on the other hand, could rattle off his favorite musicians along with their wives' names and where they lived. He had many hobbies. He enjoyed golf and art galleries. David could fill his spare time easily with things he enjoyed doing.

"I need a hobby," Natalie said to Barley.

She didn't know where to begin. A few weeks before, she had searched the internet for a list of trending hobbies, and it had overwhelmed her.

*

"Tufting?" Natalie said to David who was listening to an album in the living room. "As in rugs? People are making their own rugs? That's insane!"

David laughed. "It's quite popular, actually. I think it's cool to have whatever rug you want."

She leaned back in her chair and looked around their rental home.

"What kind of rug do you think I could put against these beige walls?" she asked.

*

They had been married for some time and still, Natalie didn't know what he saw in her. She was so plain compared to him. He was filled with inspiration and a love for art and music and things that moved him.

Natalie liked information. Even the books she read were factual. She liked books that told horrifying true stories of terrible crimes or escape from a war-torn country. Natalie had tried to read fiction before, when she was much younger. Her college roommate had twisted her arm into trying a vampire romance novel.

She had read it and cringed too many times to count—her last attempt to read fiction. Natalie knew that she was boring. Some days she even bored herself. In that sense, perhaps the beige walls suited her perfectly.

"You're only on your second cup of coffee now?" David's voice pulled her from her thoughts.

His sudden appearance frightened her, and it felt as if her lungs had dropped into her stomach. For that brief moment she'd been so separated from reality that she'd felt entirely alone in the world. It took a minute for her vision to widen from a pinhole and her heart to settle before she could answer.

"What?"

David checked his watch. "It's well after lunch time. You usually have it much earlier than that."

She checked her own watch. He was telling the truth. How long had she been at her computer? Or had she been daydreaming for too long? She sipped her coffee; it was still hot on her tongue. She couldn't have been standing there too long.

"I got distracted, I guess," Natalie said. "But I finished my portfolio."

David smiled widely and kissed her on the cheek. "I'm so proud of you for that. If you'd like, I'll take a look and tell you what I think?"

"Oh no," Natalie said with a laugh. "You're too harsh a judge. I don't think I want to know what you think."

"I'll be kind, I promise," he said.

"No thank you," she laughed. "I'm just going to use it as-is and wish for the best."

"Sure. So, have you sent it off to anyone?" he asked.

She swallowed her sip and didn't say a word. That was all the answer that he needed. David sighed and poured his own cup of coffee.

"I responded to Amanda," she said.

The muscles in David's back tensed as he paused with the mug halfway toward his mouth.

"Why?" he asked. "You don't have anything to offer her."

"I know," she said softly. "But I was thinking about how difficult it must be for her to go through that. I mean, if you went missing, I'd be a mess. I feel bad for her. So, I just let her know that I don't know anything. I offered her sympathy."

"I don't think you should have done that," David said. "She doesn't need pity, she needs information. I don't think you were helping her much."

His mood dramatically changed. She wasn't sure if it was to do with her response to Amanda, or the fact that she made no progress in sending her portfolio out. The smile had fallen from his face as he sipped his coffee. He kept his eyes cast away from her.

Natalie let out a desperate sigh. She didn't know what to do to make things better or to get herself out of the depressive hole she was in.

"How is it going with your commercial?" she asked.

David shrugged. "Same old. This one's for car insurance. It's not bad, but I'm not sure what the dance number is there for."

"Ads don't need to make sense," she said. "They just have to be memorable and slightly less annoying than the ads of the competitors."

"I suppose."

He was making conversation with her, but she knew that he was frustrated. There was a certain way in which his eyebrows settled when something annoyed him. It was a subtle sign, but she knew it when she saw it. Natalie was in no mood for another argument. There was only so much that their relationship could possibly handle.

As the hours passed, David's mood didn't change. Natalie hadn't submitted her portfolio, either. Instead, she found herself lost in a wormhole of video tutorials about crocheting.

By the time late afternoon came around she knew just how to crochet a bag, if she had the tools to do it. David reappeared for his last cup of coffee for the day and was still quieter than she liked.

Natalie felt as if she was walking on eggshells.

"What's going on?" she eventually asked, when she realized that his mood was not going to lift. "You've been off since our last cup of coffee."

"It's just work," he said. "This client is a little difficult. They're constantly going back and forth on what they want and what they like. It makes my job impossible to do."

Natalie eyed him closely. It wasn't like him to get that worked up over a job. He'd always had a fantastic ability to shed work stress, merely laughing it off.

"Are you expecting a late night?" she asked, hoping that he wasn't.

"Probably," he answered vaguely.

He left it at that and closed himself back in his office. Natalie was once again forced to face the reality that she had nothing to do that day. She took Barley for a walk, and he fought with her the entire way. Once she returned from their walk, there had been takeout waiting in the kitchen for her. So, she and David would not be sharing dinner together.

He was locked in his office, still.

Natalie searched through her overloaded bookshelf for something to read. She could convince herself that reading was an integral part of her job, and that she needed to do it if she was going to be any good at editing.

She settled on a true-crime book about a young boy who had kidnapped his neighbor and hidden her in the basement of his family home. She hoped the horrors between the pages might help her unwind.

Once she read so much as to develop a headache, she went back to her computer and refreshed her inbox. She wasn't sure what she was expecting to hear back. There was no reason for Amanda to reach out again, but Natalie wanted to know more. It might have been an interest developed from her idleness.

There was nothing from her.

There was, however, a blog to edit. Natalie let out a small sigh, happy for the small amount of income that gave her, and started working on it immediately. As she worked through the sentences advising readers on the best way to keep their lush green lawns, she thought again of the writings Alan had sent her.

She loved doing his work because he had written so descriptively. There were nights she'd imagine she was the woman he'd written it for. Amanda was lucky to have known a man with so much romance in his heart. She must have been the subject of his writings.

"Working?" David asked when he finally reappeared.

"Yeah, but just about done, unfortunately. It would be nice to receive something longer to work on sometime," she answered.

"Will you be coming to bed then?" he asked.

His bad mood seemed to have dissipated. He smiled at her and came to rub her shoulders.

"Did you get your work done?" she asked.

"I finally have a direction they like," he answered. "I'm only halfway through the commercial though."

"Working weekend?"

"The curse of being self-employed, isn't it?"

Natalie chuckled. They had spoken about her going back to standard employment, and both decided against it. The problem with being self-employed for so many years was that she had eventually become unemployable, unwilling to fit in with standard work environments.

She followed him to their room where they crawled into bed, Barley at her feet.

"You'll get work," he said as he settled his head into his pillow. "I know you will."

"I hope so," she said quietly. "Otherwise, that cardboard box is starting to look like a realistic option."

David wrapped his arms around her and pulled her in. He was all she had in the world. On days when his mood got between them, she felt lonely—until she was in his arms again, then all was forgotten.

"As long as you're in it," he said. "It'll still be home."

He was asleep almost instantly, along with Barley. Natalie was once again left alone with the chaos of her own thoughts.

CHAPTER FIVE

"I THINK I SHOULD get some crochet hooks," Natalie said as David joined her in the kitchen. "Something to keep me busy."

"Okay. What will you crochet?"

"I don't know, maybe a bag or something?" she said. "I could do with a few more cardigans too."

David nodded. "Not a bad idea. Anything else planned for the day?"

"Other than refresh my inbox and wait for a response from Amanda? Not really," she answered.

He clenched his jaw. "I don't know why you replied to her," he said. "I mean, we decided there was no point."

"No, *you* decided that," Natalie said. "Is this what upset you yesterday?"

"That was a *client*. I told you that." The snap in his response suggested she was right.

"You know, why does it bother you that I replied to her? She's struggling, and she reached out to me."

"She's dragging you into something that has nothing to do with you."

"You know that," she argued. "And I know that. But she didn't. Not until I replied. I just don't understand why this is so upsetting to you."

"I'm trying to protect you, Nat," he said. "We both know you've been struggling with the move. The last thing we need is for a woman like Amanda to come along and add to your stress."

"A woman like Amanda?" she repeated. "You have no idea what kind of woman she is. Neither do I. I just told her I don't know anything. That's all. It's not as if I've invited her to come over for coffee."

"Alan's been missing for how long?" David asked. "And she's only reaching out now? It's just odd to me. I think she's trying to scam you."

Natalie rolled her eyes. "Scam me by investigating her husband's disappearance?"

"I won't be surprised if she comes back asking for money to aid her investigation," he argued. "The timing just doesn't make any sense to me."

"Do you hear yourself right now?" she asked. "We're talking about a woman who is grieving and worried."

"Do you hear yourself?" he returned. "We're talking about a man you never even met. You owe Alan and this Amanda woman nothing."

Natalie leaned against the kitchen counter. It seemed it was time for their daily argument, which meant it was time for Barley to make his appearance in the kitchen. He came to sit down at Natalie's feet, placing himself between her and David.

"And here's the dog again," he said, waving his arms about as if it were a dramatic theatre scene.

"You know I don't like it when you talk about him like that," Natalie snapped. "He's not just 'the dog.'"

"I'm still recovering from the last nip he gave me," David said. "Face it. *The dog* hates me, Nat. He's bitten me how many times since we started dating?"

"Three," she answered.

"And he's looking at me as if it's about to be four," David said. "Last night he started growling at me when I turned over in bed. In my own bed! It's ridiculous."

She took a deep breath and held it for a moment. The argument had turned to the topic she liked the least. The last time they had argued about Barley, it had been because Natalie refused to give him up.

"He'll warm up to you," she said. "Just give him some time."

David huffed. "Sure, whatever you say."

"Don't be like that," Natalie said. "All I did was tell the woman I didn't have any information. You're behaving as if I gave her my social security number and access to our bank accounts."

"You know what? I don't have time for this," he said. "I have a commercial to finish."

He took his coffee and, as usual, disappeared into his office. The door shut behind him and Natalie knew she would not see him again for hours. She rubbed her temples as she tried to decompress.

It didn't make any sense. Had she missed something? She did often—most of their arguments stemmed from her misunderstanding something he said.

"Natalie, when will you learn?" she whispered to herself.

Barley moved from her feet and placed himself between her and the office door. It made her smirk. The only time she wasn't bothered by Barley's behavior toward David was when they'd been arguing.

"I think today's a good day to get out of the house, don't you think?" she asked Barley.

He tilted his head and twitched his ears. She had no reason to hang around. There was no work for her to do that day, and David was in another mood.

So, she got ready for the day, piled Barley into the car, and headed into town. With a warm cup of coffee in hand, she stared into the window of the crafts store. The plan had been to buy some crochet needles and yarn, but now that she was there, she knew it would be a waste of money. She already had a box in the garage somewhere filled with previous attempts at new hobbies. Natalie would be smarter this time.

There was a bookstore just next door.

"Wait here," she said to Barley, tying his lead to a nearby post.

She never had to worry about him. Barley was always well behaved—other than when David was around.

"Morning," the checkout clerk sang as Natalie stepped inside.

"Hello," she answered.

Natalie bypassed all the new releases and fiction shelves and headed straight for the true crime section. She sipped her coffee as she scanned over all the books she'd already read, then gazed upon some fresh ones.

The exact spot where she stood was where she and David had met. She'd been drinking that exact kind of coffee at the time, too. He had walked right up to her and said hello as if she had always been his destination.

*

"Hi," her nervous response came out, barely more than a whisper.

"What do you think the chances are that I can guess your favorite book?" he offered.

He towered over her, tall with dark hair and a large build. Natalie's face tilted up toward him. It had taken her a moment to comprehend what he was saying. She had expected him to ask her for a recommendation, or to ask her to move so he could reach a book he was eyeing.

She didn't expect him to set up a challenge.

"What?" she said with a laugh.

"I'm serious," he said. "I can guess your favorite book on this shelf, but before I do it, let's make a wager."

Natalie frowned. Everything about the situation had tickled her. She sipped her coffee as she eyed him out.

"What kind of wager?" she asked.

"How about this," he said with a cheeky smile. "If I get it right, you'll go out to dinner with me. On a date."

Natalie had almost choked on her coffee then. "What?" she spluttered.

"Come on, I'm not that bad, am I?" he asked. "Take a chance."

"You're a stranger," she said.

"Not if I can guess correctly," he argued. "If I get this right, then I'll know you better than you think. I promise you'll like me."

She glanced around to make sure she wasn't being pranked. Outside the door, Barley's head raised, and he stared at her intently through the opening.

"Alright," she eventually relented. "If you get this right, we'll go to dinner. But I get to choose the place."

David grinned widely. "Deal."

He turned his attention immediately to the bookshelf in front of them. He glanced across all the titles and authors. His hands brushed over the shelf, and she knew then he had lost the bet.

Then, he lowered his hands. Her breath caught when he pulled out a book with a familiar title and cover.

"*You'll Be Gone in The Morning*," he read the title. "This must be it."

Her copy of that book at home wasn't nearly as neat. Some page corners had been dog eared, and the pages were riddled with bright yellow highlighter. There were coffee rings on the cover and the back page was splashed with red wine.

She was in awe. He handed her the book, but she was too shocked to take it. How had he gotten it right?

"So then, where shall we go for dinner?" he asked.

Natalie swallowed hard. She was at a total loss for words.

"Perhaps we'll go to your favorite spot, then," he said with a wide smile. "Let me guess. The little Italian deli at the end of the street?"

She was convinced then that he was an angel—or something similar. She never believed those were real, but it also wasn't supposed to be possible for a stranger to know so much about her.

"Who are you?" she asked.

"David," he said, holding his hand out for her to shake it.

"I'm Natalie," she introduced herself.

"That's a wonderful name," he said.

"How did you guess all that?" she questioned him.

David shrugged. "Deduction," he answered. "My aunt used to be one of those scamming clairvoyants. She taught me how to read people. I was going to ask you out anyway, but I thought I'd make it fun."

Natalie wasn't sure what to think, but she was desperate for someone to get to know her. He already knew more than he should have, but he had given her the most exciting experience she ever had in a bookstore.

"It's a date then," he said.

"Do you want to take my number?" she offered.

"Meet me at the deli tomorrow night at eight," he instructed her. "If you decide to show up, I'll get your number from you then."

"What if I don't show?" she asked.

"Then I will have to count my losses, won't I?" he answered. "I really hope you show, though."

With that, he walked away from her, and she was alone at the shelf again. She noticed he didn't put the book back on the shelf. She watched him purchase it, and he gave her one final smile and wave before he walked out the door.

She was stunned. It took an entire twenty minutes before she was able to continue her shopping, by which point her coffee was cold. Natalie gathered a few books to purchase and piled them up at the cash register.

"That was odd, wasn't it?" the cashier asked.

"You saw that?" Natalie asked. "Could you hear it, too?"

"Yeah," the woman answered. "So, are you going?"

Natalie shrugged. "I don't know. I'm not sure if I should be swept off my feet or creeped out."

"Are you kidding?" the cashier asked. "That was like something out of a romance novel. You *have* to go. Stuff like that never happens!"

"I don't read those kinds of books," Natalie confessed.

"Well, if you did, then you'd know that the handsome tall gentleman who spoke to you today is your main character," she explained.

Natalie sighed. "I'll think about it."

"You don't have to go any further than just dinner if he's not for you. If you don't go, don't you think you'll regret it?"

"Probably," Natalie said. "That was interesting, wasn't it? I wonder if dinner will be the same."

CHAPTER SIX

THEIR DINNER WAS BETTER than their first meeting. Natalie laughed more than she'd laughed in years, and David had taken a deep interest in who she was. She was officially hooked.

David was the perfect gentleman. While they had agreed to move slowly at first, it wasn't too long before they confessed their feelings for each other. From that moment, things moved quickly.

Within months, they were married and living together. It had been the greatest adventure of Natalie's life. Nobody had ever come to know her as well as David.

They had a small wedding at the courthouse. For witnesses, they paid two people off the street to wait with them and sign the paperwork. Then, they celebrated on their own with a short honeymoon in Bali.

"I promise I won't let you leave me," he teased, and she'd never felt more secure.

They remained in the honeymoon phase for some time. In the end, it was her failing finances that snapped them into reality.

What followed was the most difficult thing that Natalie had ever experienced. Everything she'd ever done on her own multiplied in difficulty with marriage.

She wasn't used to having anyone other than Barley to worry about. Natalie had dreamed for so long not to be lonely anymore, only to discover that being lonely may have been a simpler way to live.

*

When Natalie pulled back into her driveway, she glanced at the stack of books on the passenger seat. She would have to sneak them in. David had already mentioned her growing stack of unread books the last time they had argued about their finances.

She wasn't ready to enter the house yet. The opportunity to truly be on her own for a while didn't come often, and she wanted to make the most of it—the only downside to being a couple that both worked from home.

Natalie backed her car back out of the driveway again and headed toward her favorite area to walk Barley. A nearby park had a forest path. Barley hopped eagerly out of the car and Natalie fixed the strap of his leash around her waist.

They headed off into the dense trees. The ground was still damp from the previous day's rain. She inhaled the scent of the damp forest floor and listened to the quiet around her. Because of the wet ground, her footsteps were silent.

They were alone on the path that day. She walked slowly as Barley sniffed everything they came across.

Natalie had never brought David to that forest path. He never had the time to go with her, anyway. He spent most of his day working in his closed office, but it hadn't always been that way.

When they had just been married, David had plenty of time to spend with her. They would go out for lunches and dinners all the time. They would buy tickets to parties and events, living carefree.

Once a month, they would go away for the weekend. Sometimes they would check into luxury resorts, and sometimes they would camp out in the mountains. They hadn't done any of that since Alan's disappearance.

Natalie waited for Alan to return, and when he hadn't, she and David had fallen into financial trouble. They had spent their savings on their honeymoon, and once they missed their first mortgage payment, they knew they were in trouble.

As Natalie walked through the lush forest, she remembered how she had cried when the paperwork to sell her home was signed. Then, when they browsed rentals within their budget, she had cried again.

She hid those tears from her new husband, wanting to make sure she didn't worsen the difficulties they were going through. She had cried often while walking Barley along this very path.

They didn't go out for lunch or dinners anymore. No weekends away were booked since their move. David worked all the time to support them, while Natalie struggled to pull herself out of the hole she was in.

At the end of the path, she sat on a bench. Barley sat at her ankles. Small birds chattered somewhere in the treetops, and from a nearby creek, she could hear frogs and toads in song.

The air was still cold after the previous day's rain. It created a suitable mood for Natalie's solemn attitude. Barley lay down and licked at a nearby tree root. She wanted to sit there for the rest of the afternoon. And she would have if she could, but she and David had promised that no matter the nature of their argument, they would not go to sleep without resolution.

Natalie wasn't sure how to resolve the morning's argument, though. She wasn't convinced she had done anything wrong, and so she didn't know how to make things right again.

Was that what marriage was supposed to be? A sequence of alternating laughs and arguments until one of them died? That was how it felt. Natalie's parents had been happily married, but they'd often argued, too.

Then again, they had not married the way she had. They had known each other for years before they had even started dating. Her parents had done everything the right, expected way.

Natalie sighed. She sometimes wished she could ask them for advice. Then, when she thought about them more, she changed her mind. Her parents would never have approved of David. Likely, if they were still around, there would only have been further family arguments.

Her mother had wished for a grandchild, but Natalie had never provided her with one. She had always worked so hard that she felt she had no time for children. That had frustrated her mother to no end, though her father had agreed.

Barley whined and tugged on the leash.

"Alright," Natalie said softly. "Let's head back."

Barley dragged her back down the path, and with excellent timing; soft drops of rain started to fall again. Unlike the previous day, when the cold rainwater had amplified her misery, it now made her feel awake. It brought her back to Earth and out of her soaring thoughts.

David provided for her when she could not provide for herself. She needed to be patient with him. He was working harder than ever to make sure they could afford their life and rebuild their savings.

Natalie felt guilty then for being difficult that morning. Of course he was in a bad mood. He worked all day with no time to unwind. Meanwhile, she struggled to get anything done and did nothing but complain about her life.

She recalled the day they got married. He had worn his favorite suit, and she had worn a cocktail dress her mother had bought for her one Christmas past. That was one of the few times Natalie ever needed to dress up.

"Are you sure about this?" David had asked.

"Definitely," Natalie answered, ignoring the nervous flutter in her stomach. "Are *you* sure about this?"

"I've never been more sure of anything in my life," he answered. "I'd do anything for you, Natalie."

If Natalie was entirely honest with herself, marriage wasn't what she expected it to be. She had imagined a successful couple, touring the world together as they grew their careers. Instead, she was the plain wife of a successful man and neither of them ever went anywhere—the future she had always feared the most.

They weren't long into their marriage, and already she was having doubts. She often wondered if David felt the same. She wondered what things would be like if she had skipped his invitation to dinner.

Natalie pulled into her driveway for the second time that day, and this time, she turned off the ignition. She moved the stack of books out of sight underneath the passenger seat.

Barley gave her no struggle that day to get out of the car; he was already eager for his afternoon nap, and the rain outside was gentle. Natalie closed the door and turned toward the house. Music filtered through the air from inside.

A wave of relief washed over her. If there was music, then David was in a better mood, and maybe even done with his work for the day. She checked her reflection in the car window and fixed her hair before starting toward the front door.

She swung the door open and stepped into the music. There was a clattering sound from the kitchen, and when she stepped inside, David was wearing the same charming smile he had on when they'd met.

"I was hoping you'd be home soon," he said eagerly.

Natalie looked around at the kitchen. The scene was vastly different to what she'd walked away from that morning.

CHAPTER SEVEN

THE MOOD IN THE house was brighter. David's favorite jazz album was filtering through the air. He was in his pajamas already and his office had been closed for the day.

The house had been tidied, and she could smell a fragrant candle burning. David hummed along with the music as he tossed some garlic into a frying pan.

"What's all this?" Natalie asked, looking around her. There was a small posy of flowers on the table and the wine was already opened to breathe.

Outside, the sun was already setting. David walked around the table and kissed her softly, his hand on the small of her back. It disarmed her completely.

"I hope you're in the mood for steak," he said cheerfully.

Natalie slid onto the chair at the kitchen table. "With fries and salad?"

David nodded. "And pepper sauce, of course. I wouldn't serve it to you any other way."

Natalie glanced at the bottle of wine waiting for her at the center of the table.

"Is this ready?" she asked.

David glanced and nodded. Natalie poured herself a glass and took a sip. She wasn't sure what to make of his change in mood. She had been prepared to apologize for something she didn't think she had done wrong. But David was behaving as if nothing happened, so her ideas had gone right out of the window, carried away by the brewing wind.

He clearly felt guilty for what had happened earlier that day. He was cooking her favorite meal and had opened up a bottle of her favorite merlot. Natalie looked at him silently and his shoulders dropped.

"I'm sorry," he said. "I think I was out of line this morning. It was such a silly argument. They always are."

"You *think*?" she asked. "All I did was send a harmless email."

"I know," he said with a sigh. "I'm sorry, nonetheless. I feel awful. I came out to find you and apologize but you were gone. I found your note on the table." David chuckled. "I got a fright for a moment. I thought you'd left me entirely."

Natalie smiled. "I'm not that easy to get rid of."

"Good. Me either," he said.

The house felt like a home again, despite the lifeless walls. Her antique furniture seemed to stand out like a hideous, sore thumb against the modern features of their rental home when the space was flooded with light.

However, with the only source of light being a candle and the strip lights above the stove, everything felt more in place.

"I'm just not sure why it made you so upset," she said. "Surely you realize I'm too smart to be scammed? I'm just trying to help her."

"I'm sorry," he repeated. "I feel horrible about it. I really do. I'm just feeling a little stressed, that's all. It's no excuse, I know that. My client has been on me about every small detail since yesterday and I guess I just snapped."

"How can I help?" she offered. "What can I do to ease your stress? I feel I need to help you in some way, and I don't even know where to begin. Some wife I am."

That was the first time she'd ever confessed to him that she felt like a subpar wife. She immediately wished she could take it back. The last thing she wanted was for him to know that she had any doubts within their relationship.

"You're an excellent woman and a brilliant wife," he said. "I have been a difficult husband. *I'm* tough to have around the house lately. I know that."

It seemed they had come to the end of their loop again. They would fight, spend some time apart, then talk, make up, and move on. Surely, it wouldn't be long before they'd start again.

She looked around at the effort he'd made and decided to enjoy this phase while it lasted. She'd always liked the way he looked while cooking. David had a way of flipping the dish towel casually over his shoulder while holding a glass of wine in one hand.

He moved as if he was dancing between the table and the stove. The food smelled incredible, and after her walk, Natalie was eager for it.

"Where did you go today?" he asked.

"I went to buy crochet hooks and yarn," she reminded him. "But I didn't buy any. I chickened out and ducked into the bookstore."

David spun around and smirked at her. "Where have you hidden the books then?"

Natalie sipped her wine and tried to hide her guilty grin. It was no use. David held her gaze and she knew she would break into laughter soon enough.

"Beneath the passenger seat," she confessed with giggles.

David threw his head back with laughter. "You don't need to hide them anymore. I've taken on some more clients. You can buy however many books you want. Besides, I get a text every time you use the credit card, remember?"

She relaxed a little. "Do you have the time for all that work?"

He shrugged. "I can always make the time somehow. I'm not sure how, but I will."

Natalie didn't like that. He was already working more than he should. He was going to burn out, and she wasn't sure she had the energy to cope with that.

David plated their food and slid hers across the table toward her. Her stomach grumbled as she looked at her plate.

"This looks incredible, thank you," she said. "I'm starving after my walk today."

"I'm glad you're hungry," David said. "When did you last eat?"

Natalie hadn't even thought of eating that day. The thought hadn't crossed her mind at all.

"I had some coffee today," she explained.

"So… last night?" he asked. "Nat, that can't be good for you."

"Don't worry," she said, sipping her wine. "I'll be right as rain after this."

David reached out and took her hand. She was eager to feel his comfort. Instead, he turned her palm up.

"Look at your wrist," he said. "You've been losing weight consistently since the move. I mean, even your tighter pants are sitting loosely on you."

"I'm fine," she said, pulling her hand back toward her.

That was the last Natalie wanted to speak about her weight. She was aware of her thinning figure. She stared at it each morning when she looked in the mirror. She felt the weakness in her muscles when she lifted Barley into the air.

She took a bite of her steak in silence. If he was going to talk about her weight, then she was going to remain quiet. It was too soon to start another cycle.

"Why don't we go away for a weekend soon?" he asked.

Natalie swallowed her bite. "Can we afford it?"

"All this hard work I'm doing, I need a break. So do you. We can go camping. It doesn't have to be anything extravagant."

She didn't know if she had it in her to be closed in a tent with David. She wanted a weekend away, but she wanted it on her own. There was no way for her to say that to him, though. Any money she spent was technically his.

"Tell you what," she said. "If I can land a new client—a decent one—then we can celebrate with a camping trip."

He smiled. "I like that kind of goal. It will make for an extra happy weekend, won't it?"

"I don't think I'll be able to relax otherwise," she said.

"Then again, when have any of our camping trips been relaxing?" he asked.

Natalie filled with laughter. He had a point. If it wasn't storming when they were camping, there was always another complication. One weekend, they got their car stuck and had to wait six hours for help.

"Do you remember the spider?" he asked.

"How could I forget?" she chuckled. "I've never seen such a huge spider. It was right by my head. I was about ready to burn our entire campsite down."

"I was happy for Barley that night," David laughed. "He snapped that spider up and swallowed it before I could even think of what to do."

"Ugh," she groaned. "So gross. I was convinced he'd be sick."

"Nah, he's a beast. Our spider defender."

That was typical of David. When he was in a bad mood, he had a problem with Barley. In a better mood, he acted as if they were best friends. Some days, the back and forth could be stressful. Other days, Natalie found it entertaining. That depended entirely on how much wine she'd had.

Natalie poured herself a little more and helped herself to a few more fries. One thing was indisputable: the meal he had cooked for her *was* helping her unwind. The further along the night went, the more at ease she felt.

Once their meals were done, David slid his chair closer to her. She sat in his arms as they sipped on their wine. Barley was fast asleep as they listened to album after album.

Natalie yawned so widely it made her a little dizzy.

"You know, I think I might actually be able to sleep tonight," she said, covering her mouth as another yawn greeted her.

"That will be good for you, you've been far too stressed out lately," he said.

"I'm just fine," she argued.

Natalie's speech slurred. She glanced toward the bottle of wine and saw that it was empty. She'd obviously had more than she thought.

"Shall we call it a night?" David asked with a smile.

Natalie nodded, a third yawn stretching her jaw.

David got to his feet and held his hand out to her. "Let's get to bed, then," he said.

She dragged her feet after him. As hard as she tried, she could not stop her yawning. Even when she pulled on her pajamas, it felt labored. She bounced softly as she collapsed onto the bed.

David placed the covers over her and pulled her into his arms. Her head was heavy as her eyes fluttered closed.

"I'm sorry," David whispered in her ear. "Tomorrow, I'll be better. I promise."

She was too sleepy to give any response other than "Mmm."

The world faded as Natalie slipped into a deep sleep. Every tense muscle in her body eased as she fell into her dreams. That night, she slept so deeply she never moved. It was the kind of deep sleep she hadn't had since she was a child after a long day at the beach.

CHAPTER EIGHT

THE SUN HAD NEVER been so bright. Natalie's head spun as she lifted it from the pillow.

"Ow," she whispered, covering her eyes.

She had a pounding headache, and the sound of blood rushing in her ears deafened her. One quick glance at the clock told her it was nine in the morning. She'd been asleep for twelve whole hours.

"Surely not," she said, reaching for the clock.

She brought it closer and double checked the time she read on the screen. It was true. She really had slept for that long. Natalie rolled her head from side to side to stretch her neck muscles. The house wasn't as quiet as she expected. For the first time in a while, she could hear the television going.

David wasn't in his office.

It felt for a moment as if she had woken up to a different life. She sat for a while as she waited for the effects of a good night's sleep to seep in. Everything felt great soon enough—except for her head. The pounding in her head only worsened.

She dragged her body off the bed and into the living room. It was nine o' clock in the morning, and David was still in his pajamas, his dark hair a mess.

"There you are," he said with a broad smile. "I'm sorry I didn't wake you. Seemed like you needed the rest."

She squinted at the screen, her head aching more and more with each passing moment.

"Judge Judy?" she asked.

"Yeah," he laughed. "It's silly, but I like it."

She raised her hand to her head. "Ah," she said in pain.

David bolted up. "Headache?" he asked.

"A killer," she said with a nod.

He was at her side in a moment. "Come sit down with me", he said. "I'll get you some coffee and a painkiller." He led her to the sofa where he propped her up against some pillows.

On the screen, Judge Judy reprimanded a fabulous woman for her knack of being remarkably dim-witted. Natalie closed her eyes and listened to the sounds of a happy, relaxed morning in her home.

"Here," David said as he pushed a hot cup of coffee into her hands. In his other hand he held a glass of water and a headache tablet—all of which she accepted eagerly. She rested her head back on the sofa as she waited for the pounding in her head to subside.

By the time it did, Judge Judy had moved onto another couple who were suing each other over a broken deck of cards and a cat with Parkinson's. David had his hand rested on her leg.

"What day is it even?" she asked.

"Friday," David said with a smile. "And a beautiful one at that. No rain predicted for today."

"Did you give Barley his breakfast?" she asked.

"I did," David said, clearing his voice. "He wasn't too impressed with me, but he was hungry enough to accept."

She glanced over at Barley who was curled up in his bed, fast asleep. Had everything in the world suddenly corrected itself just because she'd had a full night's sleep?

"Friday," she repeated. "There should be another blog post in. It won't take me long to finish. Then, maybe we could go out and enjoy the sun?"

Natalie felt calm for the first time in quite a while. David had seemingly fixed all that was wrong with the world with a good meal and a decent night's sleep in his arms.

She felt no regrets about her marriage then. In the end, all they needed was some quality time together.

"Just a few more minutes," David said, pulling her in. "You've only just recovered from your headache."

She rested her head against him as a man on the screen presented evidence of his house a mess after an unwanted party had been thrown there.

"I didn't know you were a Judge Judy fan," she said with a giggle.

"It's my guilty pleasure," he answered. "It helps me unwind. At least I know I don't have to deal with the nonsense these people do."

"True," she said softly.

When the episode ended, she moved over to her desk, only a few steps away from where she'd been sitting.

"It feels rather nice to have you here while I sit down to work," she said. "You can keep me company and listen to my ramblings when I come across something silly in the—"

Natalie stared at her screen in disbelief. Her wallpaper was gone, as were all her folders. Nothing looked the way she had left it before.

"What is it?" David asked.

"My stuff," she said, clicking around. "It's all gone. This is all wrong."

"What do you mean it's all gone?"

"It's gone!" she shouted. "All my work files and all my apps are just missing. My email isn't installed. There's nothing here."

David moved over to her side and took the mouse from her. He moved the cursor across the screen and clicked everywhere she had clicked before, as if somehow by some miracle, when he did it, the result would be different.

"That's odd," he said.

"Odd?" she asked. "It's a problem. There's nothing here. All the work I did for Alan, all the blogs I've been editing. Everything is gone!"

"You don't have backups?"

"Yes, I have some old backups, David," she whined. "But the drive is probably shoved down in the bottom of a box somewhere in the garage beneath a lifetime's worth of stuff."

She sank her head into her hands and took a deep breath to calm down.

"I'm sorry," she said. "I didn't mean to snap at you like that. It's just... this is bad."

"Let me help you," he said. "We'll get your email set up again and get it restored as best we can, okay? Maybe this weekend we can look for your hard drive."

She nodded. "How does something like this happen, anyway?"

Natalie had never been particularly tech-savvy. The sales consultant had talked her into buying the computer she had, and it was certainly more than she needed. There were features she had never tried or needed, but she got her job done. At the time, that was all that mattered.

"I don't know how this could have happened," David said. "But we'll fix it."

Natalie exhaled slowly. "It's not that bad, I guess. I'm just a bit surprised. Will you be able to get all my documents and things back?"

"I don't know," David said. "I'll do what's possible."

Everything she had worked on for Alan had simply vanished from her life. All she had left were a few pages she had printed out to edit in the old school style with a red pen. But those were packed away somewhere too. It was truly as if he had never existed. Natalie waited patiently as David grumbled and typed in passwords. In the meantime, she fixed them both some coffee and turned down the volume on Judge Judy's angry tirades.

"Alright," David said. "Your email should be ready to use, but—oh, that's odd."

"What?" she asked nervously.

"Your inbox is empty," he said.

Natalie stared at the screen in disbelief. "That can't be possible, surely. That's online and stuff."

"It's all gone. There's nothing in your spam or trash folders, either," he said.

She didn't know what to think. "David, how does this happen?"

He leaned back and pulled his fingers through his hair. "I don't know. This is really odd."

Natalie was happy to have some painkillers in her system to calm her.

"What are you going to do?" he asked.

"I don't know," she answered. "I'm going to try not to cry and hope to all that is holy that everything will be alright."

"That may be your only choice," he said.

She didn't like that option very much at all. But she didn't know what else to do.

"Well, normally I would have a blog post waiting for me in my inbox," she said. "I guess I'll just write to them and ask them to send it again."

David moved from her chair, and she took his place. It took her all of three minutes to type out the email and send it, and that was all she could do for that day.

"My portfolio," she said quietly. "There's nothing left of it." The thought made her feel sick to her stomach.

"Why didn't I just backup my work again?" she whispered.

"Don't be so hard on yourself," David said. "Nobody really does that. It's tedious. And honestly, clean wipes like this are unheard of."

"Apparently not," she said, motioning to her computer. "What the hell am I going to do now? Years of work and nothing to show for it. No way of proving that I am qualified to do my job."

"You don't need any of that to write your book," he said. "I still think the world deserves a story where a cursed woman falls in love with the devil."

"I feel like a cursed woman," she said.

"That would make me the devil."

Natalie smiled at him. "The devil couldn't possibly cook a steak so well that it put me into a twelve-hour sleep."

"Write your book," he said again. "But maybe after our picnic, because that sounded like a lovely idea."

Natalie looked at her computer. There was nothing to do. She felt helpless, and David was offering her an escape from it all for the day.

"Alright," she said. "But first, I need another cup of coffee."

"A third one? That's an addiction," he teased.

She held out her empty mug to him and waved it around. "And this is your final warning," she fired back.

Despite all that had gone wrong that day, she was doing her best to remain in a better mood. She didn't want a repeat of the previous day with David. He deserved a better experience from her, and she was determined to give it to him.

The moment he left to refill her coffee cup, her head dropped. She fought back tears that burned at the back of her eyes. There was nothing left of her except for David then. Her only client had left her, vanished into thin air. Her entire career's worth of work had been erased from her life, too.

"Hey," David said, peeping at her around the corner. "I'm really sorry that this has happened."

"It's not your fault," she said softly. "It's nobody's fault."

"We're going to be alright," he assured her. "I promise you, okay?"

She nodded, but she wasn't entirely sure she believed him. She wanted to believe him without question, but that wasn't in her nature.

"I'll pack us a picnic," Natalie said. If all she had left was David, then she would do everything in her power to make sure that she didn't lose him, too.

That afternoon, they laughed like they had when they had just started their marriage.

They teased each other, explored the park, and fed each other fruit as they basked in the sun. Barley kept them company, snuggling up at Natalie's feet and nudging David away from her.

She forgot all about her computer for a while. By the time they returned home, she really did believe everything would be alright.

CHAPTER NINE

AFTER THEY RETURNED HOME, Natalie and David sipped wine as they read. They sat propped up against opposite armrests of the sofa while their feet intertwined with each other's.

Natalie had retrieved her hidden books from beneath the passenger seat of her car. David had chosen something from that pile, too.

"How do you read so much of this and still sleep at night?" he asked.

"I *don't*. You've seen how late I lie awake."

"Is this what you're thinking of?" he questioned. "That's rough, Nat. You need to read something happier."

"I don't like reading fiction. It has too few rules," she said.

"Yet, you intend to write it?"

He had a point. One she hadn't quite considered yet. "Maybe that's why I'm having such a difficult time with it," she confessed.

David smirked. "You're going to have to learn to break the rules a little then," he said. "I think that's exciting."

"I hate to say it, but maybe I should read some fiction then."

"I could make some recommendations," he offered. "I read your favorite book. Perhaps you'd like to read mine?"

Natalie reminded herself again that David was all she had left. "I'd like that," she said.

David rose from his seat and shuffled over to the bookshelf. The shelf was just behind the sofa, with little space to move between them. That was the only space they had for it.

He reached for a book she had seen every time she glanced at the bookshelf but never seen him read. It had a horrendously bent spine, and the edges of the covers were tattered beyond belief. It was in such poor condition that even a second-hand bookshop might turn it away.

"I'm sure you can tell," he said, handing her the book. "But I've read this a whole bunch of times."

She took it from him and, for the first time ever, actually paid attention to the book. The title read *Grace and the Wolf*. The title was accompanied by imagery of carriage wheels and woodfires among large hardwood trees.

"What's it about?" she asked.

"Just read it," he urged. "I promise you, there are no vampires."

She cast an eye along the spine. It wasn't a particularly long read, two hundred pages at most. She placed her book aside and opened the one he'd handed her. For the next three hours, she was stuck between the pages, unable to put it down.

David wafted in and out of the room from time to time with a proud smile and a snack for her.

The story was compelling and strange. A woman had her life changed after she met a wolf in the woods. The wolf claimed to have known her for longer than she'd known herself and told her stories to prove it. The woman then agreed to follow the wolf to a place of safety. Along their way, they came across enemies she'd never known through a treacherous path she'd never been down before.

Natalie read as the woman and the wolf fought through trials and escaped bright burning trees, all for a goal that the main character didn't seem to understand. And the wolf had offered her no explanation.

The woman trusted the wolf blindly, because he had proven he knew her.

When the book was done, Natalie felt unfulfilled. Not because the story was poorly written or unenjoyable, but because the author seemed to have made the choice to leave all loose ends untied.

"What do you think?" David asked.

Outside, the sky had already turned dark. Natalie put the book aside and sighed.

"It's cruel," she said. "I went on an entire journey with them, and it led me nowhere."

"But Grace is happy," David said. "And she didn't leave much behind. Don't you think it is a story of freedom?"

"She nearly died a few times on her way there though, didn't she?" Natalie said. "There were fires and rough paths. And the wolf… he was just a stranger."

"Well, sometimes strangers turn out to be the best people for you," he said, raising his glass to her.

"It's an odd choice for a favorite book," she said. "But I think I enjoyed it."

"You think?" he laughed.

"I finished it, didn't I?" she asked. "If I didn't like it, I wouldn't have bothered."

He nodded. "That's fair."

They spent their evening finishing the bottle of wine as an action movie of David's choice flashed across the television screen. Natalie didn't want to say it out loud, but she could not stop thinking about the book David had given her.

How was it possible that a book with no real ending, and no real purpose to the story, could captivate her so much? It made her think of her own book. She had no outline left after her computer had been wiped. Perhaps that was a blessing in disguise. She could start again.

"Will you give me another book tomorrow?" she asked.

"What?"

"Another fiction book," she said. "Will you give me another one? I think it will help my writing."

"Of course," he said, excited. "This time I promise you it will have a proper ending."

"And no vampires."

"No vampires," he promised.

Natalie glanced at the bottle of wine. She'd drank just as much as the night before, but didn't feel half as tipsy. She had hoped it would help her sleep well again, but that didn't seem to be the case.

When the credits of the movie rolled across the screen, she was still wide awake. David, on the other hand, had puffy eyes and a drooping head.

"I'm going to work on my book a while," she said.

"I'll wait here for you," he answered.

When Natalie stood up from the sofa, he stretched out and made himself comfortable.

"I don't know how long I'll be," she said. "It could be hours."

"Wake me up when you're done, then," he offered. "Then we can crawl into bed together."

"Alright," she chuckled. "If you insist."

As usual, within moments he was breathing deeply and had fallen asleep. She turned on her computer and the first thing she noticed was the icon telling her she had an unread email waiting for her.

She opened her inbox and saw there were two. One was the blog post that she still needed to edit. The other was from Amanda.

Natalie glanced back to make sure that David was still sleeping before opening it.

```
Natalie,

Thank you for responding, I wasn't sure you would.
It's interesting that you did, and I'd like to explain
to you why that is. However, that might be tricky to
do in this manner.

Would you meet with me? Alan often spoke of you
fondly, and I'd love to meet with you and tell you
all that has happened.

Let me know which day suits you best.

Regards,
Amanda
```

"Huh," Natalie said, louder than she meant to.

She read the email again, trying desperately to remember the wording of the previous correspondences. There was one part of the email that stood out and tickled her curiosity.

She read it a few more times as she tried to decipher what it could mean. Maybe nothing, but it could also mean everything. Natalie leaned back in her chair and stared at the screen for what felt like minutes.

"What is it?" David's voice eventually startled her.

Natalie read the email out to him, and he sighed.

"It's sounding more and more like a scam," he said. "She's going to either kidnap you and sell you off to some rich mafia lord, or she'll present you with a pyramid scheme that could—according to her—make you rich."

David still had his eyes closed. She thought of the previous day's argument. She was desperate to get through one day without one.

She left it at that, reading the email again.

Then, in an attempt to distract herself from both Amanda and her book, she worked on editing the blog post. However, that work was done far too quickly, and she was faced again with what she'd been avoiding.

Natalie reopened Amanda's email. She glanced back at David, who was snoring lightly then. Then she clicked "reply."

She tapped her nails against her desk as she thought of what she would say. David had mentioned that his next big project landed Monday morning. That meant that he would be closed in his office all day.

Amanda,

I'd love to learn more about what is going on. Are you available on Monday afternoon around lunch time? We can meet anywhere of your choosing.

Natalie

She sent the response before she could change her mind. She watched as it went from her drafts folder to her outbox and then to sent. David stirred a little on the sofa and she flinched, worried he might have been peering over her shoulder.

Natalie wasn't going to tell him about her plans to meet with Amanda, as it would only make him angry. After the brilliant day they'd had, she didn't want to risk turning it sour.

Natalie opened the document in which she intended to write her new book's outline and watched the blinking cursor. After forty minutes, she knew there was no use. She had no inspiration left.

All she could think of was the email from Amanda, and what it could possibly mean.

Natalie glanced at the time. It was almost one in the morning. She was about to get up from her seat and head to bed when she saw a new message in her inbox.

Natalie,

Monday lunch time is perfect for me. I'm glad you have agreed to meet with me. It is important.

I'll let you know the address closer to the time.

Regards,
Amanda

Natalie closed the window as quickly as she could and let out a short breath. Something about it all scared her. She wasn't used to such drama in her life. She moved over and placed a hand on David's shoulder.

"David," she said quietly. "Let's go to bed."

David opened his eyes just a crack and looked at her. He brushed his fingers through his hair as he lifted his body off the sofa.

"How'd it go?" he asked with puffy eyes.

"Poorly. I wrote nothing," she sadly confessed. "It seems I am in need of much more inspiration than I thought."

David put his arm over her shoulder as they shuffled toward the room, Barley taking slow steps behind them.

"That's alright," he said. "You'll get there eventually, and I'm sure it's going to be amazing."

She pulled open the covers and helped the sleepy David into bed. He mumbled that he loved her before he was fast asleep again. The house was deadly quiet—even his breathing seemed shallower than usual.

That was a problem. When the house was quiet, Natalie's thoughts were deafeningly loud. That night, all she could think of was Grace, and the wolf who had led her thought chaos for no apparent reason.

Natalie tossed and turned until the first morning birds burst into song, at which point she settled into a semi-deep sleep lasting only three hours.

CHAPTER TEN

THE WEEKEND FLEW BY in a blur. Every few hours, David added another book to the growing stack of fiction she intended to read. Natalie's desk was filled with scraps from her notebook where she'd scribbled out basic plots just to cast them aside again and toss them in the bin.

Even just the sight of her desk started to make her feel nauseous. She didn't start her computer out of fear David would find the email and see she'd agreed to meet with Amanda.

"How's it going?" David would ask every few hours as he popped around at her desk.

"Same as always," she would answer with despair.

David would then sigh, and offer her some food or drink, and return to his own project in the garden. He was attempting to repave the walkway from the driveway to the front door.

Natalie didn't like the idea of them doing anything to improve the house. She had no intention of staying very long at all. She hated the building they were in. David had twisted her arm into it when he'd pointed out it was the only home in their budget that had enough space for Barley.

"How's it going?" he asked again as they sat down to share a pizza.

"Not well," Natalie said. "As it turns out, I really have no idea what I'm doing."

"I saw a video on this once," David said. "You're supposed to take your character, decide who they are and what they want, then you need to put something in the way of that. Something to throw off their journey."

"That makes sense, until you look at your favorite book," Natalie said. "*Grace and the Wolf.*"

"What about it?"

"What was it that Grace wanted?" she asked. "She went on a journey, sure, but what exactly was it that got in her way? The wolf or the obstacles? There was no purpose to her going through any of those things."

"I suppose," David said. "Maybe that's why it's such an enjoyable story."

"Hmm," Natalie said with a smirk. "It doesn't follow your blueprint, though. The one you learned from the videos."

He swallowed his bite. "Alright then, let's start at the basics. Who is your character?"

"An adventurous woman in bright clothes," Natalie said. "She's not particularly afraid of a challenge, and will do anything for an adrenaline rush."

"She has to be afraid of something," David said. "She's obviously not afraid of death, so a threat to her life wouldn't work."

"She's afraid of routine," Natalie explained. "The mundane sides of life. You know, school runs and nine-to-five workdays."

David chuckled. "That's a reasonable fear to have."

That was as far as Natalie had gotten. She had one barely pieced together character to work from. Her character didn't even have a name.

"Rich woman?" he asked.

"Rich enough to do what she wants," Natalie explained.

"So, what is it she wants, then?" David asked. "What would be her goal in this story?"

She tapped her finger against the table as she sunk her teeth into a slice of pizza. What would a woman like that want from her life? Someone who did everything she wanted and had enough money to do so.

"Perhaps she dies and regrets it," Natalie said. "Maybe once she had died, she wants to live again so that she can climb the one mountain she didn't climb or have a family or something."

"That's good," David said, waving his finger through the air. "So then that's how she meets the devil?"

"Yeah, I guess."

She dashed to her desk to get her notebook so that she wouldn't forget anything they'd been talking about. She scribbled it all down on a new sheet of paper. This time, she was certain it wouldn't go missing.

"So then, what stands between her and a second chance at life?" David asked.

"Perhaps the devil himself," Natalie answered. "He might be the only person who can offer it to her, but in that regard, he can keep it from her too."

"So, she needs to prove to him she deserves it?" David asked.

"Something like that, yeah," she said. "Or perhaps she needs to pass some tests, or survive some intense trials before she deserves a second life."

"Write that down. That's good!" David said.

"I'm going to have to add you as a collaborator!" Natalie teased.

"What if she develops feelings for the devil along the way?" he asked. "Toward the end, she must choose if she goes back to her life and gets to live again, or she can stay with the devil, and they can enjoy each other's company."

Natalie nodded. "That's complicated. I like it."

He smiled. "Good. I told you the formula works."

"Yeah, yeah," she said. "I know the formula. I'm an editor, remember? Sometimes it just helps to bounce ideas off another person."

David was being more supportive than he'd ever been before, and she wasn't sure where that was coming from. He had assured her multiple times that weekend that their finances were improving, and due to only improve further in the coming weeks.

He had promised her that as soon as they could, they would buy an old house somewhere. Something she could fix up as she pleased. They felt like a happy couple again.

"I need to work on this," Natalie said, tapping the tip of her pen against her notes. "I better get this down today before it slips from my mind."

"Well, if peace and quiet is what you need, then don't worry about it. I need to pick up some groceries anyway. So, I'll be gone for a while."

Natalie smiled. As soon as David was out the door, she went to sit in front of her computer again. She opened a document, and a basic outline came flowing from her fingertips. Almost all of it was inspired by David's ideas.

Then again, he had read a lot more fiction than she had.

It only solidified to her that David was the best thing that had ever happened to her.

She typed quickly and with ease as she outlined the characters of her book and the world it was set in. She then decided on three acts that would make up the book, and how long they would each be.

It was as if a faucet had been opened in her mind. Inspiration and productivity poured out of her.

Within an hour, she was ready to start outlining each chapter. Then, she saw an unread message in her inbox.

```
Natalie,

If you would, meet me at my home tomorrow.

208 Acacia Drive.

I'll let you in when you get here. I hope you like
wine.

Regards,
Amanda
```

The sound of David's car pulling into the driveway caused a slight panic within her. Natalie quickly shut down her computer and stepped away from her desk.

"Need some help with those bags?" she offered, doing her best not to sound nervous.

She hated hiding stuff from David, especially something so important. Something they'd already argued about. Her mouth was dry, and her hands threatened to tremble.

"Sure, thanks," he gladly accepted.

"That took ages," Natalie said, filling the space with pointless conversation. She knew that if it fell quiet, her nerves would only get worse until she could not hide the guilt on her face. If David became suspicious of something, he would ask her what was wrong, and she'd cave. Then their blissful weekend would be ruined with another argument.

"The queues were longer than I'd anticipated," he said.

"On a Sunday?"

"There was a special on baby formula," he explained. "Mothers and children everywhere."

"Ah," Natalie laughed.

The kitchen table was filled with bags, and she continued the small talk as they unpacked—until it could no longer be maintained.

"How did it go?" David asked. "With your book? Did you get anything done?"

"Yeah!" she said with a bright, forced smile. "The characters and the summary."

David reached into a bag and produced a bottle of champagne. "Then buying this was no waste."

Natalie laughed. "It's hardly worth that kind of celebration."

"Of course it is," he said with a grin. "It's the start of something great. That's always worth celebrating."

She gave in. In the short time they'd been together, she was quickly learning to let David take the lead on most things. Perhaps that was why it felt so wrong to go against him by agreeing to meet with Amanda.

"I'd love to read it," he said softly. "What you've got written down, that is."

Natalie froze for a second. If he was going to read it, then he would have to sit at her computer to do so. That gave him access to her emails. While she didn't think he was one to snoop, she worried he might simply see something by accident.

She'd never had other serious relationships, and she didn't know how to behave while lying to a partner. She twirled her wedding ring nervously around her finger as David poured their champagne.

"Not yet," she said. "There are still a few details I want to add, and then you can read it. I'll be more comfortable with it then."

"I won't judge," he said.

"I know, but still." That was her best counterargument.

David narrowed his eyes playfully. "Fine, but promise me you won't delete it."

"I promise," she smiled.

For the rest of their evening, they sipped champagne until the bottle was empty and until their heads were spinning. When the sun set, they left for their bed.

They tied themselves up beneath the sheets, tangled in each other as they made love that night. With each turn of their bodies or kiss on her lips, she knew she was sinking deeper into something she did not understand.

The better he treated her, the worse she felt about lying. David had always been nothing but honest to her, and now she was keeping secrets from him. After everything they'd already been through.

When he touched her, he did so with the assumption that she was an honest and caring wife, but she knew different. When he kissed her, he did so as if there had never been anything wrong between them... but she knew that was false. Natalie played along, though. She couldn't upset the peace.

That was the cruelty of keeping secrets. It would subtly rot every good moment until it was all over. Natalie needed to decide if she could live with that—and if David deserved it.

The champagne and the lovemaking should have made sleep an easy friend that night. By the time they came to a stop, Natalie was entirely out of breath and could hardly tell which way was up.

Yet, by the time David's heavy breathing slowed, Natalie was wide awake again. She stared up at the ceiling and pondered her life.

What would David think of her if the truth came out? Was *she* the wolf leading him through tests and trials for no apparent reason?

She decided then she would tell him, but only after she'd been to see Amanda. He would be angry, but then she could stop the rot before it was too late.

CHAPTER ELEVEN

THE CAR FELT LIKE a small, moving prison. Natalie's stomach turned and twisted with each passing minute. Amanda's home was over an hour and a half away, and the closer Natalie got to it, the more she felt too afraid to go ahead with the meeting.

If she wasn't already more than an hour in the right direction, she might have turned back. Although, the thought of doing that continued to tug at her. Natalie didn't know what Amanda could want or get from her, and she hated that she was keeping it from David.

As far as he was concerned, she was going to spend the day somewhere in nature to think about her career and her book. It felt wrong. So wrong that Natalie felt ill. More than that, she'd deleted the entire outline document for her book that morning. She hated it. It didn't feel right.

Eventually, she opened every window of her car for some airflow. She felt as if she had a small fire blooming in the pit of her stomach. When she glanced in the rearview mirror, her cheeks were pink.

Stress had never sat well in Natalie. While she coped, the physical signs were sometimes debilitating.

"Get it together," she whispered to herself.

Another chance to turn back came by—a slipway that would turn her back in the direction of home. She could go back and spend time in nature.

She drove past it and watched the chance to turn back disappear behind her. For the entirety of the drive, she went back and forth in her mind in that manner until it was too late.

The voice from her GPS startled her out of her thoughts, letting her know her destination was coming up on her left. Natalie swallowed back the fright she'd had and rolled up the windows.

208 Acacia Drive showed up on her left, and she pulled her car into the driveway. As the house came into view, Natalie felt as if the nerves she'd carried with her solidified into lead and weighed down inside her.

The house was vast. Modern, and nothing like the kind of life Natalie could ever have—or want, for that matter. She felt ridiculous arriving there, as if she had anything to offer to a life so different and separate from hers.

"I should have turned back," she said quietly.

No amount of talking to herself was going to help, though. She was already there, and it was too late to change it. Besides, there was a lot she wanted to understand for her own reasons. Natalie hoped Amanda might have some of those answers for her.

The house was so different to everything in Natalie's life. Everything was a stark gray colour with modern finishes. Steel beams and metal window frames. Every single plant in sight was perfectly manicured and vibrant green.

It created a feeling in Natalie she couldn't stand. She felt out of place, as if she didn't belong.

She glanced in her mirror and felt instantly worse. Driving with the windows open had taken what was once a neat and presentable hairstyle and turned it into something that seemed fresh off a windy boat ride. There were stray strands of hair everywhere.

Natalie ran her fingers through her hair in a desperate attempt to neaten it up. She wasn't the kind of woman who carried a comb in her handbag, and at that moment, she wished she was.

There wasn't much she could do, other than push most of her hair behind her ears and hope it was passable.

There was no more time to waste. Natalie clambered out of the car, her handbag snagging on the steering wheel as she did. If anyone was watching, she looked like a total mess.

With a shallow, slow breath, she tried to find a place of calm and collectedness to approach the house.

She stood at the front door, aware of the contrast between her and everything that represented Amanda, and her bravery wavered again. The door was a large, perfectly treated steel door that loomed in front of her. Already a small woman, Natalie felt like a mouse compared to the house she was about to enter. This was her last chance to turn around.

She tried not to think about it. She pushed back the familiar feeling of inadequacy and straightened her back. It was the least she could do to aid her first impression.

When she rang the bell, the sound echoed through the house. It had only occurred to her then that she might have been walking into a trap, as David had warned. How could she be certain the person in the house was even Amanda?

Perhaps it was a complete stranger, and she was about to be kidnapped and sold to the highest bidder. Everything she had ever been warned about regarding strangers on the internet came flooding to her mind.

Her heart leaped into her throat, fluttering, making her dizzy. She was frozen with fear as the sound of footsteps approached. How could she be so foolish? She was doing precisely what everyone had always taught her not to do—and told no one she was doing it.

David didn't know where she was. She was alone and vulnerable.

The footsteps were almost at the door as Natalie considered running away. She glanced back at the doorbell and noted that it had a camera attached. Whoever was inside had already seen her.

Her nerves were making her irrational. Why would someone go to such lengths to get to her? That was an outrageous thought, she figured. Her hands were trembling by then, though, and she could feel sweat gathering in the small of her back.

The heavy door opened easier than Natalie anticipated. On the other side of it, a tall woman welcomed her in with an eager smile.

"Natalie?" she asked. "I'm so pleased to see you. I'm Amanda."

The woman bypassed a handshake and went straight for a quick hug.

"Come in, come in!" Amanda said, waving Natalie in the right direction.

Amanda towered over her. Her clothes matched the gray, minimalist appearance of the house, and her straight black hair hung like a stark line all the way to her hips.

"I'm glad you came," Amanda said. "I've got a place set up on the patio—is that alright?"

"Oh," Natalie said, relieved by her friendliness. "Yes, of course."

Amanda glanced back at her. "I like your shoes," she said.

Receiving a compliment from a woman like Amanda felt ridiculous to Natalie, but she stammered a thank-you and followed her through the house. Every wall had large windows and clean, simple furniture.

On the patio, a glass table awaited them with a view of rolling lawns and lush, maintained gardens. There, a man waited for them with his arms crossed and a face unamused.

"This is Charles," Amanda explained. "He's the private investigator I hired. I hope you don't mind. I thought it might be good to have him here."

"Not at all," Natalie answered, although his presence certainly ramped up her nervousness. "I suppose that makes sense."

"Great! Amanda ushered her to the table. "It's a perfect day for the garden."

"This is beautiful," Natalie said, taking in the scenery.

"Isn't it?" Amanda asked as they took a seat. "I can't think well if things aren't exactly how I like them to be."

"Maybe that's my problem," Natalie said. "My home is a little chaotic at the moment. Could explain some of my decisions."

Amanda chuckled. "Don't get me wrong, I still make bad choices. It's just that here, I feel okay about it."

Natalie wasn't sure where to start the conversation. They were strangers, with one questionable person in common, and Natalie was still mildly concerned about being kidnapped.

"Are you alright?" Amanda asked. "You look a little worried."

Natalie forced a smile. "I'm alright," she said. "I guess, the circumstances are just a little weird."

"That they are," Charles said sternly.

A woman arrived, in a grey uniform, and placed a pot of coffee on the table with three mugs.

"I hope you like coffee," Amanda said. "Otherwise, Sarah can bring something else?"

"No, coffee is fine," Natalie said, eagerly accepting a mug.

"I'll get right to it then," Amanda said. "As I explained in the email, Alan has been missing for some time. The police are totally useless, and I have few leads to go on."

Natalie nodded as she filled her mouth with coffee, hoping to use it as an excuse not to respond yet. It worked.

"I'm doing the best I can, but things take time," Charles said. "Speaking to people usually moves things along."

"Before he vanished, Alan was distant," Amanda continued. "He started to shut down, and evenings in our home became quiet. I'm convinced he was getting bored with me like he had with his previous long-term relationship."

"So, you were having problems?" Natalie asked.

Charles clenched his jaw.

Amanda seemed perfectly comfortable opening up, despite the two women being strangers. Natalie envied her confidence.

"I would assume so, although he never said anything," Amanda answered. "He always insisted everything was fine and he was just tired from work."

Natalie nodded. "I would often get work from him at all hours of the morning. I was convinced he worked through the night, most nights."

"He did," Amanda said. "I've never known anyone to function on as little sleep as he did. Perhaps that made him angry, I don't know."

"Why are you looking into this now?" Natalie asked the question that had been burning in her mind for ages.

"The case has been ongoing," Charles explained. "But as Amanda mentioned, the police investigation went nowhere. I'm making good headway with all his devices—phone and laptop and such—but I'm afraid it's taking longer than I'd hoped. The police only recently handed over what little information they had."

Natalie nodded as if she had extensive knowledge about such things.

"In the beginning, I suspected he'd simply left me," Amanda said. "I mean, toward the end, he was like a stranger. I barely saw him a few minutes a day. It was a horrible feeling. When he didn't come home after a few days, I assumed he'd bailed out of our marriage."

Natalie looked around her. "And leave all this behind?"

Amanda chuckled. "He was never into *stuff*. He was into his business, and that's it."

"My husband can be the same way," Natalie said softly.

Amanda lit a thin cigarette and puffed the smoke into the air, another neat grey against the modern backdrop.

"You're married, then?" Charles asked, but she suspected he already knew the answer.

"Yes, fairly newly married," Natalie answered, hoping their struggles would not be evident in the expression on her face.

"No divorce papers ever arrived," Amanda said. "And there was no money removed from our accounts after he disappeared. So, it's safe to assume he didn't just leave me. I mean, nobody we know has heard from him again. That's a difficult thing to pull off, and I'm not entirely convinced he *would* have done it if he could." Amanda watched Natalie closely.

"Alan and I worked together for years, but I knew nothing about him," Natalie explained. "I was surprised when you reached out to me. I mean, I never even knew his last name."

"Really?" Amanda asked. "I mean there were thousands of texts between the two of you."

"Yeah," Natalie said. "His writing needed a lot of work. Our contract was under his business name, so his full name wasn't listed anywhere there. After your first contact with me, I thought about it some more. I never even knew where he lived or what other work he was involved in. But I don't ask anything like that about my clients."

"So, he just sent you work, and you did it?" Amanda asked.

Natalie nodded. "Yeah. That's often the nature of what I do."

"Sounds blissful, honestly," Amanda said. "People are complicated. Sometimes, minimizing interaction beyond what's necessary is the best thing to do."

"Did Alan ever let you know to stop working?" Charles asked, his brows furrowed deep.

"No, he simply stopped reaching out," Natalie explained. "I sent an edited document back to him and never heard back. He always paid in advance, so I didn't think much of it. I just thought he had decided not to use my services anymore. In fact, it really affected my confidence in ways I'm embarrassed to admit."

Amanda offered her a supportive look, but it did nothing to make Natalie feel better about herself.

"I wish I could be of more help to you," Natalie said. "In truth, I'm not sure why I agreed to meet with you. I'm afraid I might be wasting your time."

Natalie glanced to see how much coffee she still had left to drink and Charles cleared his throat. She had a fair drive home, and it was clear Amanda was a busy woman. How else could she afford that house? It made Natalie feel like a fool to waste her time that way.

CHAPTER TWELVE

THE MORE THEY SPOKE, the more at ease Natalie felt. Despite her perfect appearance, Amanda seemed perfectly willing to share her faults.

Still, there was a piercing look in her eyes that made Natalie feel as if she could peer right inside her.

The house and garden were quiet, and it felt as if they were miles away from anything else. Natalie attributed Amanda's calm and confident demeanor to the peace that surrounded her.

Eventually, Sarah returned with two glasses of water and a platter of fresh fruit. It felt less like a home and more like a hotel, but it seemed to be the way Amanda liked it. The fruit was cold and perfectly ripe, and Natalie wondered for a moment if she was perhaps dreaming.

It all seemed a little too perfect. Natalie tried to control it, but she couldn't stop her head from turning as she took in all the details of the space around her.

"Some people say my home is a little cold," Amanda said, catching her eye again. "I can see where they're coming from. I like it this way. I can be a bit of a germophobe, I admit."

"It's impressive," Natalie said. "It's quiet."

"Yes, the architect made sure that the roof trusses were positioned in such a way that it dampened sound and eliminated echoes," Amanda explained. "Some people think it's over the top."

"Not at all," Natalie said. "I think I've just been in my little cottage so long I've forgotten that there's a world outside of it.

Amanda offered her a kind smile. "That sounds like a nice, quiet life."

Natalie didn't know what to say. How could she tell Amanda that she hated her new life and sometimes imagined leaving it? She couldn't. Amanda was a stranger, and it made no difference to her.

"The business name on the contract…" Amanda said. "I think it was Pathway Pages or something, right?"

"Pathfinder Pages," Natalie corrected her.

Amanda nodded. "I'd never heard of it," she said. "I knew of his other three businesses but not that one."

"I was under the impression it was his only business," Natalie said. "Not because he said so. As I said, he hardly said anything personal to me. It just never occurred to me that he might do anything else. Not at the rate that he wanted work done."

Amanda nodded. "That's what I was thinking, too. If I may ask, though, what kind of books were you editing for him?"

"They were mostly travel stories," Natalie explained. "Fiction books. You know… adventure and romance."

She reached for another piece of fruit. Amanda's eyes left her for a moment and stared off into the distance.

"A business might be a way for us to trace the money," Charles said. "That could give us another lead."

"I guess I was of some help after all," Natalie said sheepishly.

"He never traveled," Amanda said softly. "I tried to get him to go on vacation with me multiple times, but he always refused."

The air between them seemed to shift. Their energy tensed. Natalie no longer cared about her appearance, or how out of place she seemed and felt. Something was wrong. She didn't know what to think about it.

"He seemed to be so passionate about it, and wanted every detail to be correct," Natalie said carefully. "I always assumed he traveled often and that some of what he wrote was from personal experience."

"Did the books do well?" Amanda asked.

Natalie shrugged. "I don't know what happened to them after I was done with them. I never knew the final title or the cover... anything, really. It felt a bit odd, but he paid well, and he gave me consistent work."

"That's fair, I guess," Amanda said.

It was clear Amanda's mind was racing with thoughts and possibilities. Natalie wasn't sure what else she should ask about, and what was better being left alone. She opted for silence. It seemed best to allow Amanda to lead the conversation.

"He was an odd man, I suppose," Amanda said, still deep in thought. "I shouldn't be so surprised by the odd nature of this conversation."

"Once we get into his computer, we'll get answers. I'm sure of it," Charles said.

"I'm sorry, I don't know what else to say, really..." Natalie confessed. "If I'm honest, I'm not sure why I came here today. I don't really have anything to offer you."

"You've offered plenty," Amanda said, leaning forward. "Alan was always good at business. If he was creating books and selling them, I can be confident it was profitable. Especially considering he continued with it for so many years, while having no real interest in travel."

Natalie swallowed hard. "That makes sense."

"So, the money he made from those publications, or potentially is still making, must be going somewhere," Amanda said. "It might explain how he's been funding himself all this time."

"I can't seem to find any evidence that the books were ever published," Natalie said. "I've been curious about their purpose myself."

Charles rubbed his chin. "I couldn't find any published works by Pathfinder Pages, either."

"When I first saw the business name, I thought it was an accounting company he was using for one of his businesses," Amanda added. "Publishing wasn't really his style."

"If he wasn't publishing anything, then we need to discover the true purpose of Pathfinder Pages," Charles said, his eyes focused on the distance as if he were unraveling the truth while they sat there.

"Do you really think he's still alive?" Natalie asked. "If he left, why would he leave his computer and those items?"

"If he's missing long enough, he'll be presumed dead and Amanda can claim the life insurance," Charles said. "I think he wanted the world to believe he died."

"Well, his car never went missing and his body never turned up," Amanda said. "It's been a few years. As I said, I initially thought he just left me. I still feel that way, but it's odd."

"Why wouldn't he just divorce you if he wanted to leave?" Natalie asked.

"That's my question exactly," Amanda said. "There has to be more to this than what seems obvious. Either that, or he really did die and I'm wasting my time here."

Natalie reached for another piece of fruit. If she was chewing, then she wasn't expected to say anything. A feeling of heaviness came over her as she understood her role in it all. She was the only link to the mysterious business that Amanda suspected was funding her missing husband's new life.

"The other question I have in my mind is…" Amanda said, pausing a moment to think it over. "Why did he go quiet on you then? You know, if your work was helping him make money."

The entire situation was starting to feel a little ridiculous. The sprawling mansion around them, Amanda's perfect appearance, the fresh fruit and coffee brought around by the housekeeper, and the conversation all seemed surreal.

"Your life is a little like a movie, isn't it?" Natalie said, wishing she hadn't gone to the meeting.

"It does feel like that, sometimes," Amanda said. "It can make it difficult to remember just how real this all is. Like my real life is a dream, and my dreams are reality."

"I suspect this will end up nothing like a movie," Charles said. "It won't be half as dramatic. As soon as we find the right puzzle piece, it'll be like the truth was staring at us the whole time. I'll get to the bottom of it, and there'll be peace for you both."

Natalie no longer felt uncomfortable. His words made her feel as if she could get the closure she needed, too. Everything about it had become so ridiculous that she was entirely at ease. She wanted to laugh and wave off everything Amanda was saying. While she otherwise had all the time in the world, she felt she didn't have the time for what was currently unfolding in her presence.

"Sometimes I wonder if he'll just come strolling in through the front door and back into my life as calmly as he left it."

"You saw him on the day he left, I'm assuming?" Natalie asked.

"I did," Amanda answered. "He was as distant as he'd been for months prior. He told me he was stepping out and waved casually at me as he walked out the door—then never returned. I can still see those last moments in my mind when I close my eyes. It looked so insignificant, but was one of the most important moments in my life, I suppose."

It was Natalie who was watching Amanda closely then.

"It's a lot to leave behind," Natalie commented. "A beautiful house, a good wife, and multiple successful businesses. That doesn't seem like something someone just walks away from."

"*Now* you sound like an editor," Charles said with a small chuckle.

"It *isn't* something you walk away from," Amanda said bluntly. "Which is why I suspect there's more to it."

"If we assume he's alive and just walked out of here, then something must have changed before he left," Natalie said. "Can you think of anything?"

Amanda shook her head. "I can't think of anything that changed. We built this house shortly after we were married. Alan liked to stick to his routine. More than that, he was often brutally honest. It's so difficult to believe his feelings toward me might have changed without him saying anything."

Looking at Amanda, it was impossible to believe that any man might change his feelings toward her. Natalie was inclined to agree that something different was going on, but she wasn't sure she wanted that level of involvement in it.

"I'm sorry about what you're going through," Natalie said in a feeble attempt to add to the conversation.

"Don't be," Amanda said, waving her off. "It's been so long now that I'm not sad anymore. I'm just confounded… and lonely."

Natalie imagined what her own life would be like if she was suddenly alone again. If David was just gone and she had to return to her old lonely routine. The thought made her feel cold, and she shuddered.

Her life might have felt difficult over the last weeks, but it was nothing compared to how devastated she would be if David simply vanished.

"I can't imagine what that must feel like," Natalie said, verbalizing her thought.

"It's odd," Amanda explained. "The first few days I expected to hear news of his death. Then as the weeks rolled by and no evidence came forward, I was just confused. And I remain confused, but now that I've spoken with you, I have a little more to think about."

"Like what?" Natalie asked.

Amanda's face fell to a serious expression. "Like how there were entire sides to his life that I never knew. Secret businesses and such. I'll have to dig deeper into the man I thought I knew better than anyone else."

While Natalie wanted nothing to do with the case, the relationship between Amanda and Alan was becoming more and more interesting to her.

"How did the two of you meet, if I may ask?" Natalie abandoned the fruit platter.

Amanda's eyes lit up. "I used to go to the same coffee shop after work each day," she said. "One day, he was there. There were no more tables, and he invited me to join his. We had a good conversation in which he learned I went there every day." She chuckled. "After that, he was always there waiting for me. He became a little obsessed with me, I'd say. It took him three months to convince me to give him my number and go on a proper date with him."

Natalie laughed. "Again, just like a movie."

"Well, in that case I'd like to see the end of it now, please. I need to know what happened."

"You need closure," Natalie said, thinking it sounded profound.

"I don't care about closure," Amanda said, making Natalie feel a little silly. "I need to know if he is alive or dead so I can do what's right with his assets. I keep waiting for him to turn up and it's becoming exhausting. Does he still have ownership of half my life? Or can I keep it all and move on?"

"Why not just go ahead and keep it all?" Natalie asked. "I mean, if he left and did abandon you, then you owe him nothing, surely?"

"That's the worst part," Amanda said, and this time her smile didn't quite reach her eyes. "I still love Alan. Wherever he is, I don't want to hurt him. I don't think I could ever really move on from him, if I'm honest. He was perfect for me."

CHAPTER THIRTEEN

"IF YOU DON'T MIND me being so rude," Natalie said. "Hearing what you've just said and knowing what I know now, Alan didn't deserve you."

It was as if saying something potentially hurtful was all that was needed for the two women to become friends. There was a brief silence before both women burst into a fit of giggles.

"I'm sorry," Natalie said with a sigh. "I had to say it. After all he's put you through, you still want to do the right thing? That's impressive."

"I'll never understand it," Charles sighed.

Amanda gave her a sideways glance, coupled with a suddenly cheeky disposition.

"Is it too early for a glass of wine?" she asked.

"I could certainly do with one," Natalie answered.

Amanda lit up. "Excellent!"

"Not me," Charles answered. "I'm on the clock."

Within minutes, two chilled glasses of white wine were on the table. Natalie had been hoping their lunch would have some form of alcohol involved. Her nerves and tense emotions while approaching the house had put her completely on edge. She wasn't sure how to behave, but hoped the drink would help.

The sound of glasses clinking together rang out over the large gardens—with no echo—and finally, it was time to unwind a little.

"So, you know an awful lot about me now," Amanda eventually said. "Tell me something about you. Until now, you've been nothing more than a name on the other end of a screen."

"Oh, there's not much to tell actually," Natalie said. "I'm married and have a dog named Barley."

"And you work as an editor," Charles added.

"Sure," Natalie offered, although she didn't feel like she could completely agree with that. However, after another sip of wine she felt she could offer Amanda the same kind of transparency she'd received.

"Actually, I used to work as an editor," Natalie said. "Since Alan disappeared, I've not had much work coming in, I'm afraid. I suppose that was partially my fault. I relied on him a little too much to keep the work coming in."

Amanda winced. "I'm so sorry to hear that. I would have thought that there'd be loads of editing work around."

"It's a competitive field as a freelance," Natalie explained. "Besides, I think a lot of it has to do with my confidence. I went down a bit of a spiral."

She had hoped to leave it at that, but Amanda met her with an expectant look, and she knew she'd have to elaborate.

"I thought Alan disappeared on me because I didn't offer good enough work," Natalie confessed. "To be honest, everything had been so chaotic with my new marriage and everything, I think I *did* drop the quality a little bit. I blamed myself all this time for it. It affected my ability to approach new clients and sell myself."

"That's sad," Amanda said. "I can tell you one thing about Alan. He only worked with those he thought were of a higher standard. So, you can let go of all that nonsense."

Natalie felt a small, very brief wave of relief. She understood where Amanda was coming from. However, it had been so long since she'd been able to successfully land a client that she still wasn't sure she could do it. It would be like starting all over again.

"You know, I'm glad I met you," Amanda said. "I have a little confession to make."

As if the air had turned to ice, Natalie's breath caught in her throat. "Okay?"

Amada put down her glass and slumped her shoulders slightly, as if relieved.

"For a short while there I thought perhaps you and Alan were having an affair," she said.

The sip of wine caught in Natalie's throat and came spluttering back up. Her eyes widened like saucers. Charles' eyes were fixated on her, as if he was waiting for her to break.

"What? Why?" Natalie choked out.

Laughter bubbled up from deep within Amanda. "Well, the first text I clicked on was one that he sent you. I didn't realize they were for books. I saw all the romantic words and imagery written out and assumed the worst. Thought he'd run off with you."

Uncontrolled laughter slipped from Natalie then. In fact, she hadn't laughed that hard in many months and it didn't stop until her eyes misted over.

"Then I kept reading, and I saw that it was something else entirely," Amanda said. "I felt a little silly. Still, for a moment I was happy to have found an explanation."

"Had you looked me up before you contacted me?" Natalie asked.

"I did," Amanda said. "I had to see what the woman who stole my husband from me looked like."

Natalie did a quick comparison between herself and Amanda and tried to imagine what Amanda must have thought when she first saw the photographs.

"That's rather outrageous," Natalie said as she caught her breath. "I'll need more wine after that one."

Without hesitation, Amanda gestured for their glasses to be refilled.

"At least now I can be sure I'm not being kidnapped," Natalie said.

"Kidnapped?" Charles had a deep frown.

"Since we're confessing our feelings," Natalie said with a chuckle. "Earlier when I got to your house, I worried that I might have fallen into a trap."

"Who was going to kidnap you? Me?" Amanda asked.

"I don't know," Natalie whined. "You're a stranger from the internet. That's literally who they've been telling me to avoid since the internet was invented. And yet, I drove all the way to your house. A person on the internet."

Amanda's laughter was so loud then that it startled Natalie.

"I never even thought about it like that!" Amanda cried. "That's hilarious. I promise you, you're not being kidnapped. I can't even imagine the kind of effort and admin that is required for something like that."

"Well, I promise you Alan and I were not having an affair," Natalie said. "He was just another stranger on the internet, too. I never met him in person."

"Yes, my concerns have faded," Amanda said, casting a close eye on Natalie.

Natalie wanted to sink into the Earth. Why hadn't she made more effort to get dressed up that day?

"Well, I'm glad I came anyway," Natalie said. "I needed that good laugh. I'm just sorry that I couldn't be of more help."

"No, I'm sorry," Amanda said. "It seems that Alan's disappearance has affected us both. Here I thought I was alone in all of this. It's good to know I'm not."

The desire to crawl into bed and let the covers swallow her up had Natalie in a grip then. The last few minutes of conversation came flooding back and it embarrassed her entirely.

"I suppose it's a little insensitive of me to complain about losing the work and the income when you literally lost the love of your life," Natalie said, her cheeks turning hot. "I didn't realize just how distasteful that might have been until just now."

"Please," Amanda said kindly. "I don't see it that way. It's not that I find joy in knowing you're struggling without him. It's just comforting to know I'm not the only person who is having a difficult time moving on from him."

"So, what will you do now?" Natalie asked.

She couldn't stay much longer. There was only so long that she could pretend to be out in nature, and she would still need to stop for a meal more substantial than a fruit platter, a mug of coffee, and two glasses of wine. Still, she wanted to know what would come next.

"I don't know," Amanda said. "I suppose I'll look deeper into Pathfinder Pages and see if I can follow a money trail anywhere."

"That's smart," Natalie said. "You should be able to get something. I'll see if I can't figure out more about the publications themselves—if that will help?"

"At this point, literally anything might be useful," Amanda said. "Charles is a real bloodhound with any detail. I'm glad I hired him."

Natalie swigged back her last few sips of wine, hoping that Amanda hadn't heard the way her stomach grumbled just moments before.

"What are *you* going to do?" Amanda asked. "You know, about your job and such?"

Natalie let out a small sigh. "I'm working on a book. Well… I haven't gotten very far, but my husband thinks now is the right time to do it."

"Do you have an idea what the book will be about?" Amanda asked.

"Not the foggiest," Natalie said. "Which, as I'm sure you can imagine, makes it more difficult. I've just always wanted to write a book of my own. I've worked on so many that I'm convinced I can do it. Only, I can't come up with one solid idea."

"I think your husband is right, you know," Amanda said. "Sometimes bad things happen, and they result in good changes."

"There's nothing good in Alan's disappearance for you," Natalie commented.

"Maybe not," Amanda replied. "But I suppose I've met you. I think you're a delightful person. I hope you'll come over again sometime soon."

"That would be nice," Natalie said.

Was it that easy to make a friend? Natalie had never really tried. Her life had been largely solitary. Then again, how would she develop a friendship with Amanda when she was keeping their entire meeting a secret from the one other person in her life?

Natalie's stomach churned as she left Amanda's house. She hadn't expected anything specific, and yet, nothing had gone the way she'd expected. It didn't make any sense, and Natalie was acutely aware of the logic leaving her mind.

The steering wheel was sticky from where her clammy hands rested. It didn't matter that she hadn't had a proper lunch, her appetite had all but left her.

Amanda had worried that she and Alan were having an affair. That meant even if it had just been for a brief moment, there was a time when Natalie was a suspect in the case. This time, she had the windows rolled up and the air conditioning on low. It was a cocoon she was after—somewhere safe and warm.

She wanted to feel Barley's soft fur and hear the sound of the mugs in the kitchen as David made himself another cup of coffee. Natalie wanted to be home, and she wanted to get there as quickly as she could.

Knowing how easily Amanda's world had been turned upside down, she promised not to take anything for granted. Natalie also made a silent promise to herself to pay a little more attention to her appearance.

If she and Amanda had any chance of being friends, then she'd need to do something about it before they were seen in public together.

"Everyone might think you're her charity case," Natalie said to herself quietly.

She glanced down at the fuel gauge and bit her lip. Going to see Amanda had been riskier than she'd originally thought. In truth, she couldn't afford to spend the fuel. It would likely cost her a few trips to the hiking trail and back. When every penny counted, she needed to budget the miles she could travel each month.

Natalie arrived home and still didn't feel as if it was all over. Guilt bloomed within her and it was quickly making her miserable. She didn't like keeping secrets.

As she arrived home and prepared to leave the safe cocoon of her car, she knew she would have to confess. She knew the sooner she got it over with, the better it would likely be—before the rot of secrecy and deception set in.

With that in mind, she took her time gathering her belongings and her thoughts. She prepared to tell him where she'd been and what she'd learned in the process. After all, she couldn't just keep it to herself.

That kind of information would come spilling out eventually. No, it was time for her to take control of the situation. She had made a decision, and she would face its consequences.

CHAPTER FOURTEEN

HER HOME WAS PEACEFUL. There was music playing from the living room again. All the windows were open, allowing a pleasant breeze through the house. It was cold, but the fresh air seemed to create a feeling of peace throughout the house.

It only made the heavy feeling in Natalie's chest feel even more so. She walked quietly to put down her bag as she considered all the ways she might open the conversation with David.

"Nat, is that you?" he called from the bedroom.

She heard the bed creak as he raised to his feet and padded in her direction.

"Hey," she greeted.

He'd been sleeping. His hair was a mess on one side, and she could see lines where the cover on the pillow had folded beneath his weight.

"I can't believe I fell asleep," he said, rubbing the back of his neck. "I only wish I hadn't put my head down on the pillow so funny. My neck is killing me."

He looked so at ease. The most relaxed he'd seemed in weeks, and she was going to upend it all. Part of her wanted to leave it for another day, but she knew that would only make it worse. The secret she kept from him would grow and fester into something larger, and the longer it was before he found out about it, the worse the betrayal would be.

"How was your afternoon in nature?" he asked.

Natalie grimaced. "I have to tell you something," she said. "I went somewhere else."

David seemed suddenly awake. "What?" he asked, rubbing his eyes. He moved over to the sofa and settled in, his eyes still on her. "Where did you go?" he asked. "You've been gone for hours."

The feeling that seeped into Natalie then was horrible. She could see all the ways his mind was going, trying to piece together what she was about to say. And she hated that she needed to confess anything to him at all.

"I had lunch with Amanda," she said.

The color drained from his face. White patches formed beneath his eyes and even his lips turned a paler shade of pink.

"Alan's wife?" he asked.

"Yeah."

Natalie wasn't sure what to do with herself. Should she sit next to him? He was clearly upset. What she really wanted to do was pace up and down and tell him everything, but she wasn't even sure he wanted to hear it.

"The woman I asked you not to go see?" he said. "Because it was potentially dangerous? Because she could have been a scammer? A kidnapper? A murderer?"

Natalie nodded. "The very one."

She could see every ounce of tension in David's body. His shoulders tightened and he clenched his jaw. Then, his hand went to cover his eyes, a clear sign that she'd given him a headache.

"Okay. Why did you go? Wait. Before that, why didn't you tell me where you were going? What if she really was someone dangerous?"

"I know," Natalie said. "The thought crossed my mind when I was standing at her front door. I'm not proud of myself."

"I asked you not to go and you did it anyway," David said. "I'm beginning to feel a little out of sync."

"I promise you, it was fine," Natalie explained. "We had lunch and a conversation. She's actually a really nice woman. *Very* fancy house."

"That's not the point," David snapped.

Natalie felt a new sensation making itself known then. It grew larger within her until it felt as if it was going to burst from her skin.

"What else am I supposed to do, David?" she argued. "Sit in this house and hope inspiration finds me? I do nothing all day and it's driving me insane. There are only so many hours of the day I can dedicate to *hopefully* getting a new client. Then I spend the rest of my time feeling depressed while you lock yourself away in your office."

Whatever peaceful atmosphere had been in the home before, it had been shattered. David reached for the remote and paused the music.

"You went to meet a stranger without telling me!" he said.

She could feel her mood darken instantly.

"I spend all day in this house alone," she argued again. "You work all the time. So much that I hardly get to see you, and when I do, it's always strained. It was nice to get out and laugh for a change."

"We spend quality time together," David countered.

"When? Once every few weeks?" Natalie asked. "You're my husband. Quality time shouldn't be a special occasion."

David rose from the sofa. "Hey, I work as hard as I do because we need to pay the bills," he said. "So we can get out of this tiny little house and back to somewhere nicer. So you can find the time to gather the courage to get more work. It's not by choice, Nat. It's a necessity."

His voice was coarse and tight as he stared her down. She tried to find something to say, but there was nothing. That was the first time she'd ever heard him sound truly bitter about their situation. It made her feel smaller, and less significant than the shadow of an ant on the dirt.

The way he loomed over her was different. It had never happened to her before, but she was afraid of him then. There was a look in his eye she couldn't recognize, and it made him seem unpredictable.

"You shouldn't have gone," he said. "Next time, try just talking to me first. As you pointed out, I'm your husband. I would think you can talk to me."

David stormed off into the bedroom and closed the door behind him, leaving a heavy and empty space where he'd been standing. Natalie felt as if she was biting at air as she tried to think of what to say, or how to make things right.

Instead, she sat where he'd been seated and sank her head into her hands.

"This isn't working," she said quietly to herself.

Then she thought about how she'd felt when Amanda had told her about losing her husband so suddenly. How sad it had seemed to wake up one morning without the love of her life there.

That wasn't the reality that Natalie wanted for herself. She'd gone her entire life with nobody but Barley, and she didn't want to go back to how that had been. The sofa groaned a little as she leaned back and rested her head.

The sound of the bedroom door opening snapped her back into reality.

"Nat," he said, his voice lowered and calm. "I'm sorry."

"*You're* sorry?" she asked with a struggled chuckle. "I'm the one who should apologize. I lied to you."

David nodded. "Yes, but I could have handled that better just now, I think. Like I said yesterday, I'm going to be better today."

"We both could have handled it better, I suppose."

He walked slowly and carefully toward her, as if she might cower from him and sat down beside her. His hand rested on her knee, and she fell into him. She focused on the warmth of his embrace and the comfort of his arms around her.

"I really don't want to fight," she said.

"Me neither," he answered. "That's the last thing I want."

Every knotted feeling in her stomach unwound and her shoulders relaxed. She was hungry again.

"I really need to eat something," she said.

"Didn't you have lunch?"

Natalie looked up at him. "She's a fruit platter kind of woman."

David smiled. "Ah, of course. I'll get you something."

She was so happy to be through with the confession that she didn't stop to consider what an odd response that had been. While she had noted it, she chalked it up to him just saying that he understood why she was so hungry.

When he returned, he had a fresh sandwich for her, and she accepted it gladly.

"So, what did she tell you?" he asked.

Natalie frowned. "Do you really want to know?"

"Of course," David said. "I can admit, the situation seems a little interesting to me, too. I just don't like the idea of you going off to meet strangers."

She swallowed. "Alan just walked out of the house one day and disappeared. There's been no body and no money out of the accounts or anything."

"Sounds like he died," David said.

"He didn't even take his car," Natalie continued. "Turns out, the company he had me doing work for was one he owned. Amanda had no idea the business even existed before she found our emails the other day."

David's eyes widened. "That's a little suspicious."

"More than a little," Natalie said. "She says he never traveled. That she'd ask him to and that he wouldn't want to do it. Yet, all he had me working on were those travel romance stories."

His finger was tapping against the top of his knee.

"A lot to think about, isn't it?" she asked.

"Yes," he answered, but his mind was far away. "So, what is she going to do now?"

"Well, she was hoping I knew more," Natalie said. "She even said that she'd misunderstood one of the romance snippets he'd sent me and thought we were having an affair. As if! You should have seen Amanda. She was like something out of a magazine."

"Doesn't matter, I'm still sure you're more beautiful," he teased.

"You have to say that." Natalie took another large bite of her sandwich. "Anyway, Amanda's going to look into Pathfinder Pages. She thinks she'll be able to follow the money and see if he's still alive somewhere."

"She thinks he just walked out on her?" he asked.

"Mhmm." Natalie nodded. "She says he was distant for weeks before he disappeared."

There was a silence in the room. Natalie watched David closely and could see that he was becoming as interested in the entire story as she was.

"You know what's wild?" Natalie asked.

"I'm sure you'll tell me."

She smiled. "Amanda says she still loves him. She only wants to figure this out so that she can do what's fair with his assets."

David snorted. "That is wild, you're right."

"I don't know, I think it's kind of sweet, too," Natalie said. "You know what else? It would make a good book, I think. Amanda could be the leading lady."

"She really made an impression on you," David teased with a chuckle.

"We got along," Natalie shrugged. "In fact, we'll probably have lunch again now that we know each other and I'm certain there's no threat. I might even make a friend. Imagine that."

"I don't know," David said. "You only met her this once. She could still be dangerous."

Natalie smiled. "Why don't you come with me next time? Then you can meet her and see for yourself."

It looked as if she had asked him to commit a murder. In fact, David seemed completely disgusted by the idea.

"No thank you," he said. "That doesn't seem like my kind of thing." He checked his watch and whistled. "I have to go," he said. "I'll be late."

"Late?" Natalie frowned.

"Yep. Online meeting. Apparently, my client has decided to go in a completely different direction… again."

"Oof, sorry," Natalie said. "And good luck. I'll take Barley for a walk in the meantime."

She watched him disappear into his office and close the door behind him. If being friends with Amanda was going to get between her and David, then she would have no more time for Amanda.

Natalie was used to being alone, without many friends. However, she was no longer used to being without David, and the thought scared her to her core. Whatever it was he needed her to do to keep their marriage stable, she would do it.

CHAPTER FIFTEEN

"I'M SORRY, BARLEY," NATALIE said, wheezing for breath. "It isn't your fault."

One too many tugs on the lead, coupled with yet another argument that afternoon had resulted in Natalie snapping at the only creature who had been her loyal companion for all those years.

She stopped to calm down and make sure Barley hadn't been hurt. The moment she bent down to pat him on the head, his face broke into a wide and friendly smile.

There was a tremble in Natalie's hands as the stress of the day—and the weeks prior—threatened her sanity. She had taken Barley on a walk in the hopes of clearing her head. Instead, she was only filled with further doubt and chaotic feelings.

What was she going to do?

She hadn't landed a new client in months and was no longer sure she knew how to. More than that, she had lost so much confidence in herself that even crossing the road seemed like something she might fail at.

Natalie waited until there were no cars anywhere in sight, even if it took twenty minutes for that moment to come.

Eventually, though, she had to turn back home and face the small desk which functioned as her office. There, she would need to figure it all out.

David was right. She had no right to blame him for the loneliness she felt in her marriage when she was the reason he needed to work such long hours to begin with. Her mother had always warned her she couldn't have it all, and that was becoming increasingly apparent.

If she wanted to spend quality time with her husband, she would need to find a way to ease his workload. If she wanted to continue on for the rest of her life without working, she would need to find a way to be comfortable going long hours without him.

Barley stepped inside and shook his fur, plumes of dust bursting into the air.

"You need a bath," Natalie mumbled, making a mental note for herself.

She hung up the lead and kicked off her shoes. That would be the last time she was going to leave the house for that day.

"Nat?" David called.

"Yeah?"

She listened again as he walked slowly toward her. When he emerged again, his messy hair and sleepy face was gone. Instead, he was still damp from a shower and half the small cottage seemed filled with steam as a result.

"Can we talk?" he asked.

Those were her least favorite words in the world, but she would do anything for them to move on from the hurt feelings they'd had earlier that day. She offered him a quick nod.

He motioned for her to take a seat at the kitchen counter, where two glasses of red wine already awaited their conversation. This time, she told herself she would try her best just to listen. She wasn't sure she had the energy for another argument. It had been a long day. She was tired, and there was still much to face.

The kitchen counter felt ice cold as she leaned against it, raising her wine glass quickly to her lips.

"I want to apologize," he said quietly. "I know that I already did, but I still don't feel right about what I said."

"About what?"

"I know you're not doing any of this on purpose," he continued. "I'm working hard, but not because you're not good enough. I don't ever want you to feel that way."

Natalie wasn't sure how to respond. That was exactly how she felt, and she wasn't sure that a few words from him would be enough to melt those feelings from her skin, where they clung to her like barbs.

"I also know it won't be like this forever," David continued. "You're trying, and you're doing your best, and all I can do is trust you. I guess I'm just starting to get tired, and it shows sometimes when I don't mean it to."

"I don't want our marriage to make you tired," Natalie said.

David offered her a knowing smirk. "Marriages can be tiring. That's just how they are sometimes. It doesn't make them bad."

"What? Have you been married before or something?"

The small amount of food in her system, coupled with her third glass of wine for the day was making her feel braver than she needed to. David's lips paled again as he stammered over his words.

"N-no," he answered. "It's just that bringing two people together, merging their lives, throwing in a bit of struggle and adding a temperamental dog is bound to make things tough."

Natalie clenched her jaw and bit back her words. The last thing she wanted was yet another fight about Barley, but she was starting to believe David simply wouldn't let it go.

He watched her closely for a moment as he tried to assess just how far he'd crossed the line.

"You can't ignore that Barley adds a layer of stress," David continued. It seemed that he wouldn't let it go without commentary from her.

"Barley was here before you," she said. "If he doesn't like you, there's nothing I can do about that."

"Nat, this morning he tried to block me from entering the bedroom while you were still sleeping," David said. "I'm surprised you didn't wake up from all the growling and arguing. That's how used to the aggression you've become."

"He doesn't do that to anyone else," Natalie snapped. "The two of you are going to have to figure that out. He doesn't speak English. It's not as if I can just ask him nicely to stop."

David sighed. "This is not the point of the conversation."

"Then why did you mention it?"

She could feel the frustration burning behind her eyes as she stared at him. She took another sip of the wine, hoping it would soothe her temper. All the seesawing between emotions that day was starting to make her feel raw, and with each added layer she felt more broken inside.

"I was merely trying to explain why I said what I said earlier," David answered.

"About me not pulling my weight? That I can't seem to land a job no matter how hard I try?"

"I knew you would take it that way," David said, his voice turning cold.

"How else am I supposed to take it?" she snapped. "Those words might have just *slipped* out of you or something, but that doesn't mean they weren't important. They were on your mind. That's how it happened."

"Nat, if we can't even have a conversation without it turning into an argument, then what are we doing?" he asked.

His words felt laced with venom, as if they could pierce her skin and burn her insides.

"What?" she asked. "What is that supposed to mean?"

"Every time I mention the dog, you take his side," David explained. "I'm expected to just be patient, to try harder, and wait for you to get your life together. The expectation is always on me. Eventually, you'll push so hard that you'll push me away."

She put down her glass. "Is that a threat?"

David rose from his seat. He looked completely defeated by her. "It's just something to think about," he said.

He waited for her response. Did he want her to beg him to change his mind? Was she really that close to losing him? It was proving to be too much.

"I need time," she said, pushing back her chair as loudly as she could. "I'll be at my desk. There's something I need to do."

She didn't know what else to do other than to brush him off. Natalie left him in the kitchen with an ocean of silence that swelled between them. She did as she said she would and made her way to her desk.

At least that way she had her back turned to the world.

Her screen brightened and lit up her face. She didn't know what to do first. There was nothing for her to even pretend to work on since she'd binned her previous attempt at an outline. She opened a new document and watched as the insertion point blinked impatiently, awaiting her first words.

Minutes passed and again, she just stared at a blank screen.

"This is stupid," she whispered, but she was far too proud to leave her desk. She opted for listing what she already knew about Alan and his disappearance.

```
Left his house
Left his wife
Left his money
Pathfinder Pages = Strange
Must be nuts
```

That was all she had. It wasn't much at all. As the writer, she could fill in the blanks as she pleased, but none of it made any sense to her so, she didn't know where to begin filling in that information.

Natalie gave up, just as she expected she would. Instead of trying again or thinking on it further, she checked her email. It came as no surprise to her that there was one waiting from Amanda.

```
Natalie,

Thank you for coming to see me today. Your visit was
helpful and left me in better spirits than I've been
in in a while. I finally have a new direction to look
at.

More than that, it was nice to speak with someone who
has also been affected by Alan's disappearance. I keep
waiting for the situation not to hurt so badly, but
it continues on. It's good to know there's at least
one person who understands.
```

Natalie let out a struggled sigh. Amanda pitied her. At least, that was how it felt. And it was the last thing that she wanted to know. To her, it seemed as if she had let everyone down. There was nobody left who had any confidence in her.

Barley bumped her leg, making her aware of his presence. She reached down and scratched him around the ears. When it had been just the two of them, things had been better. There'd been less pressure on her.

But she'd been lonely. While Barley was a good dog, and they were inseparable, he wasn't always the most fulfilling company. Her life had been deadly silent before David.

The memory of her early days with David set something off in her mind. With ease, the tips of her fingers tapped at her keyboard as she laid out the few details she knew about Amanda and Alan's first meeting. She added one more item to her list of what she knew about him.

With that, she laid out the beginnings of a story in which Alan sat each day at the coffee shop, hoping to meet with her. With each passing day, Amanda took up more space in his mind until eventually, he couldn't think about anything else.

Eventually, Alan managed to get her to join him at her table. Amanda was blissfully unaware of how much danger she was in.

CHAPTER SIXTEEN

"WOAH," DAVID SAID BEHIND her.

Natalie jumped, an unexpected profanity slipping from her. She hadn't noticed him walk up behind her and wasn't sure how much he'd read.

"What is all that?" he asked.

"It's how Alan and Amanda met," she answered. "I thought it might make a good start to the book. Although, it's creeping me out a little bit."

David glanced over the words again and swallowed hard. "Do you think it's creepy?"

Natalie nodded. "A little," she said. "I mean, he's waiting there for her every day as if she is the focal point of the day. It's mildly creepy."

David frowned. "I don't think it's creepy," he said. "In fact, I think it's a little romantic."

"Romantic?" Natalie asked. "Perhaps on the surface, but knowing about his disappearance, it seems a little odd."

"He was clearly infatuated with her," David said. "I mean, that's a lot of effort he's putting in."

"Not really," Natalie argued. "He's just showing up there each day. That's all."

"I'm sure there's more to it than that," David continued. "He probably had to change his schedule to make sure it worked. Then he had to be sure that he would get a table, so he probably tried to get there early. Never mind the days when she maybe didn't go, and he waited there like a fool for hours."

Natalie nodded. "That's good," she said, quickly typing away.

"See? Romantic," he said.

"You're not much of a romance writer, are you?" Natalie asked.

David shrugged. "No, but he was."

That made her laugh loudly. "He wasn't very good, if that's your best argument," she said. "The number of edits required were substantial, and it was largely to do with how his characters inter-acted with each other."

David mumbled something beneath his breath before walking away from her. Natalie looked back at her screen. No, she was right. It was creepy. She shut down her computer and stepped away from it, eager for a warm bath to soothe her dampened spirits.

However, the more she thought about it, the more bothered she was by David looming over her and reading over her shoulder. The home was small, but surely she should be allowed some privacy.

She wondered how he might feel about it.

With that in her mind, she headed toward his office door. That was where he had skulked off to after their last conversation, so she knew he must have been busy with some work in there.

In all the time she'd known him, he'd never shown her the results of his work. Yet, he felt comfortable peering over her shoulder and watching the start of hers? That hardly seemed fair.

Natalie pressed her ear to the door and listened. She could hear a one-second snippet going back and forth as he tried to perfect his scene.

Did she want to crack the door open just a little, or did she want to burst into the room and demand she see what he was working on? Natalie opted for the version that would give him a fright the same way he had startled her.

Natalie readied her hand on the door handle and prepared for her entrance. In a second, she pushed the handle down and burst into the room, letting in a beam of light.

She could see the screen, and a one-second snippet replaying, but David was not in his seat. Rather, he was lying with his feet propped up on the one armrest of the small sofa that was in the room, his eyes closed and his earphones in his ears.

"What?" she asked, but he didn't hear her.

She felt like a giant, stomping as she moved over to him. Her hands pressed against his feet as she shook violently. Her attempt at frightening him was successful. David pulled his feet away from her and grabbed for his earphones.

"What the hell are you doing?" she asked. "I thought you were working!"

David looked over at the screen and reached across to stop the sound from repeating.

"I was," he answered.

"You were asleep just now," Natalie said. "Literally, you had your eyes closed. You didn't even hear me come in."

"I was just resting my eyes," David said.

He was furious with her. That was obvious in the way his right eye had started twitching and he was fiddling with everything on his desk.

"With the snippet still playing on a loop?" she asked. "How could you rest your eyes through that?"

"I was watching it, trying to decide if I like it and I fell asleep," he explained.

"How?" Natalie pressed. "That sound should drive everyone insane."

"I had my earphones in," he said, as if it was the most obvious answer in the world.

She stared at him a moment, hoping he might see on his own why that statement made no sense to her at all. However, after a few minutes of silence, he still didn't seem to get it.

"You had your earphones in while the snippet played out loud over and over again and you're apparently watching it back while listening to something else?" she asked, pointing out the insanity of his own claim.

"I don't expect you to understand," he said.

"You're right, I don't understand," she answered. "Are you just in here to avoid me? Because you're quite evidently not working."

The last thing she wanted was an honest answer to her question. Natalie spun on her feet and left him there, unwilling to give into his pleads for her to come back and talk to him. Her heart felt heavy, and her mind raced with anger.

She closed herself in the bedroom and collapsed on the bed. There had never been a time in her life when she felt as lost as she did at that moment. Her career was over, her husband was avoiding her, and she had absolutely no idea what to do.

Eventually, she mobilized again and went to fill the bathtub with water. She hoped that if she could soak long enough, all the negative feelings might seep from her, and she could simply let them spiral down the drain.

Her issues were nothing that could be avoided. She let the steam in the bathroom swallow her up and hide her from the world again.

When she sank into the warm water, her muscles ached, and her head was pounding. If she hadn't been so exhausted, she might have cried. It had been the longest day she'd had in months and if she could, she would have turned back the clock and done things differently.

She might have taken David's advice and not gone to see Amanda. Then perhaps she and David wouldn't have gotten into so many arguments.

She thought of her lunch with Amanda and all that had been discussed. There had been a moment when Amanda was concerned that she and Alan were having an affair.

The bedroom door closed, and she heard the bed creak as David made himself comfortable. Natalie lowered herself until her head was completely submerged beneath the water.

There, everything was quiet. All she could hear was the sound of the water around her and the rushing of the blood in her ears. With her eyes closed, she could pretend that she was floating out on the ocean somewhere, far away from her life.

She brought her face to the surface just in time to catch her breath. Water splashed over the edge of the bath as she leaned her head back. Her life was supposed to be happy. Her husband was supposed to be a source of support, and while he *was* that, he was also an immense source of frustration.

Everything of the last few weeks came back to her. All the phone calls he took away from her so that she wouldn't hear. Finding him asleep in his office instead of working. How often had he done that?

Should she have trusted Barley's opinion of him? Her mother had always said that if a dog didn't like someone, there was a good reason. Could Barley sense something in David she couldn't?

Then again, David was the only solid thing she had left in her life. Natalie hated her home and what had happened with her editing career. The information about Alan's disappearance was only adding to her tension.

How did she wind up in the middle of something like that? And why did she get such a foreboding feeling when she thought about it? It felt to Natalie as if she was being dangled over a flame. Every day, she was lowered closer to the heat, and it seemed as if she was reaching a boiling point.

The water was cool by the time Natalie moved again. She'd been lost in her thoughts, and she wasn't sure for how long. However, by the time she was ready to get out, she was determined to change at least on aspect of her life.

If her marriage with David was going to dissolve, or explode, or whichever direction it was headed in, then she needed to be able to stand on her own. To do that, she needed to get her career back in order.

There might be a future without David in it—one where he no longer supported her, financially or otherwise. She needed to ensure she could survive without him. Alan had vanished, and Amanda was left behind. It happened to the best people, it seemed, and there was no reason David couldn't leave her one day too.

She dried herself off and pulled on her pajamas, ready to face her computer. She could write a book, and she could sell it, too. Natalie just needed to choose the right words on the page. How hard could it be? Words were what she had always worked with for a living. She was an expert with words.

She walked into the room, certain David was already asleep, but he wasn't.

"You shouldn't have come into my office like that," he said quietly. "The door is closed for a reason. I should be allowed some privacy, don't you think?"

"Like how you read my work over my shoulder?" she asked. "I might not have a door, but I deserve privacy just as you do."

"It's different and you know it," he said.

He looked as if he was going to raise his head from his pillow and prop himself up. Natalie was done talking things through with him. She had other things to focus on. Things that would benefit her, rather than break her down again.

"I'm going to work," she said. "I'll let you know when I'm ready to talk with you again."

It felt refreshing putting that boundary in place. Normally, she would allow David to take the lead, but the time for that had passed.

She made her way to the kitchen to fix herself a hot cup of tea before braving the scary monster that was her desk. As she made her way into the living room, she caught a glimpse of David's office door.

It was closed again, as it always was.

She pretended the entire room wasn't there anymore. The idea that he might have been using it to avoid spending time with her was the most hurtful idea she'd ever had to face.

Natalie took all those hurt feelings and packaged them tight within her. Then, as she typed, she allowed them to pour from her in a steady stream. Those emotions built characters and cemented scenes to the page.

She worked until her wrists ached, waiting for the time that she might hear the first morning birdsong filter through the windows.

Barley snored away at her feet, but the rest of the house was eerily quiet.

On the pages, Alan and Amanda had met and fallen in love already. He was already starting to grow distant when she decided to make herself another cup of tea. Nothing would stop her stride.

It was as if everything that had been pent up within her over the last weeks was slowly releasing onto the pages, draining from her body and mind, freeing her. When she finally stopped for a moment to read back what she'd written, she felt a sense of purpose again.

CHAPTER SEVENTEEN

HER SKIN WAS ALREADY red when she woke up. She could feel it in the tingle on her skin. The sun had been beating down on her through the window, landing directly on her face where she'd fallen asleep on the sofa.

A few bright blinks and she was able to raise her head from its resting place. She had no idea what the time was, or where David was. All she knew was that her dreams had been flooded with images of Alan—where he was and how he got there.

Only, his face was nothing but a dark space at the top of his shoulders. Despite all their years of working together, she had never known what he looked like. However, she had often put a made-up face to his name.

In her mind, he'd been blonde and little pudgy. However, after meeting Amanda and seeing the standard she had for everything in her life, she knew it couldn't be so.

There was already a pot of coffee in the kitchen with what appeared to be two cups of coffee missing from it. David had been awake for some time.

His office door was closed, but this time there was no sound from inside at all. Natalie rolled her eyes and poured her first cup of coffee for the day. The time on the oven took her by surprise. She had slept two hours longer than she usually did.

At first, felt guilty for it. Then, she remembered she had absolutely nothing scheduled for her day and let go of that guilt. She would walk Barley, work on her book, and do her best to ignore her problems until she had an idea of what to do about it.

For the first time since she'd started trying to write a book, she felt as if she was excited to continue with it. Natalie could remember what she had written the night before, and knew she was on the right path.

There was only one person she wanted to share that news with. Back in front of her screen, she took the time to respond to Amanda's email.

```
Amanda,

Thank you for the lunch and the wine, and most
importantly, the laughs. You have no idea how badly I
needed it.

I must admit, the conversation inspired me more than
expected. I finally know what I'd like to write about.
The book will be heavily inspired by what has happened
to you. I hope that's alright.

Of course, we have no facts, so it will be fictional.
I've not managed to feel this inspired since I set
```

By the time she sent the email, her coffee cup was empty, and it was time for the next. Pouring her next cup of coffee would empty the pot of coffee in the kitchen. Usually, she would have put the next one on to brew. However, she thought about what had happened the previous night: David lying on the sofa with his headphones in, pretending to work in order to avoid her. And with that in mind, she decided she would leave an empty coffee pot for him to find.

It would send him a message.

Natalie knew that eventually David would come out of his office, and he would attempt a conversation with her. Then, she thought of Amanda, a woman so impressive she had made Natalie want to cower just the day before. She was sure Amanda would never have allowed herself to be treated that way by Alan.

No, Natalie would do what David did. She just needed to find her headphones. An accessory she hadn't used in many years. They were likely stuffed in a box in the garage, like most of her things.

She took her coffee and braved the garage that had functioned as a storage room since they'd moved. Scanning the boxes, she hoped to narrow it down to at least just a few boxes. On top of the nearest box was the pair of kitchen scissors she'd been looking for, mostly used for opening boxes when they needed to.

At the back, she saw a box labeled "library." That was the best place to start. Natalie climbed through the narrow spaces between boxes—one of the few times she was grateful for her small disposition.

The box was filled with trinkets, books, and old contracts. No headphones, though. She moved on to the next box, then the next, until eventually, she was physically exhausted and mentally overwhelmed from revisiting all her old belongings.

Abandoning her efforts, she returned to her desk with the sole purpose of searching for and purchasing a new pair of headphones. However, the world of audio had come such a long way since she'd last looked. The options seemed endless, and the choices were complicated.

Each option was accompanied by a video review in which a young person used slang Natalie had never heard, coupled with vaguely recognizable technical terms.

"I just want a simple pair of headphones," she said quietly. "That's all. How can it be this difficult?"

"You have headphones," David interrupted.

Natalie didn't look at him. "I can't find them. I've already checked the boxes."

"They're in your nightstand," he answered. "I put them there when we moved in."

Natalie pursed her lips. "Thank you," she said coldly.

She would go and find them when David wasn't looking. Natalie knew she was being petty. However, it made her feel just a little better, so she leaned into it.

Instead of jumping up to find what she'd been looking for all morning, she opened her book to keep working. She checked behind her every few seconds to make sure David wasn't lurking.

It wasn't necessary, though, as she could hear him loudly clanging about to make another pot of coffee. Clearly, her message had been received. Eventually, he dragged his feet past and toward his office again.

As soon as his door closed behind him, she raced off to the bedroom to retrieve the headphones. However, once she had them, she had no idea what to listen to. So, she put them on her head and continued on in silence.

She made herself comfortable in front of her computer again and read through the last few paragraphs she'd written the night before. It was far from perfect, but it was good enough to continue. She was proud of herself for that.

She checked her outline again to see what she would write next. It seemed a little sad that there was silence in her headphones. It had been so long since she had listened to what she wanted—or enjoyed an audiobook—that she no longer remembered what she liked.

That would have to change. After everything that she'd been through, she was determined to find herself again. Natalie had given herself to David so completely that she'd abandoned herself in the process.

In her heart, she knew it would be the topic of their next conversation. She wanted them to work, to survive everything that was going on, but she needed to find herself again. And she was sure that, if David loved her enough, he would be happy to see her do it.

Natalie wrote, making sure each keystroke was loud and purposeful, so that David could hear she had started on something and that it was good. She wanted to prove to him that she could do it, and she wanted to regain control. In the meantime, though, she got a little kick out of driving him insane.

It didn't go unnoticed by her that he slid a fresh cup of coffee onto her desk, without saying a word to her. Likely, that was an olive branch. In truth, she didn't know how she was going to move past the idea that David was potentially trying to avoid spending time with her.

If she wasn't so angry with him, she might have asked him what he liked to listen to when he had his earphones in.

She sipped her olive-branch coffee and focused on her manuscript again. With her notebook at the ready, she started plotting out the next chapter in detail so that she could get it written that day.

Then, she set the scene. That chapter would depict the day Alan left the house—the moments leading up to his disappearance.

And it was going well until she saw a new email waiting for her in her inbox. It was another email from Amanda. This time, however, the subject line held a different tone.

From: Amanda Peckin
Subject: You lied

Natalie swallowed hard, nearly choking on her sip of coffee. She hovered her cursor over the email, unsure of what to expect inside. Was it some kind of joke? She hoped so, but she had a gut feeling it was something else.

Natalie,

I was so pleased after you left here the other day. You even laughed when I mentioned I once thought you and Alan had an affair. Perhaps it was foolish of me to believe you so easily, or to brush it off before.

Still, did you really think I wouldn't eventually learn the truth? I have all the evidence I need of your affair with my husband. Thankfully, I knew him well enough to finally guess the passwords to the locked files on his computer. I am now certain you know more about his disappearance than you say.

You've already lied once, so there is no reason you won't lie again. All the evidence of your affair is already being pieced together by Charles, as well as the investigating officers on the now-reopened case.

You'll be hearing from one of them soon enough.

Until then, stay away from me.

Amanda Peckin

Natalie was completely stunned. It was as if her heart stopped, and her thoughts had been wiped clean from her mind. She read the email over and over again as if the words would suddenly change and it would say something else. Her mouth dried, and the thought of another sip of coffee made her feel nauseous.

What she read was impossible. There could be no evidence of an affair, since there had never been one. Still, Amanda seemed confident.

She leaned back in her seat as she tried to piece it all together. More than anything, she wished she still had her previous emails between her and Alan so she could try and see what Amanda might have deemed as evidence of an affair.

Since that was the only way they'd ever communicated, that would be the only place the so-called evidence could have been. And why would Alan have kept it in a password-locked file?

The smell of David's deodorant pulled her from her thoughts that Natalie became aware of his presence behind her.

"An affair?" he asked.

Natalie spun her chair around. "Stop creeping up behind me!" she snapped. "You can't just read whatever you want because it's on my screen!"

"Nat, that says that you and Alan were having an affair," he said with a scary amount of calm. "What is going on?"

It felt as if a spotlight had been turned on her, and it turned her insides, twisting them into tight knots.

CHAPTER EIGHTEEN

EVERY FRUSTRATION SEEMED TO have come to a point at that moment. Natalie plucked the headphones from her ears, but it was pointless. They were ringing from the pressure she felt. David sat down carefully on the sofa.

"This is insane," she said quietly.

"Yes, it is," David answered. "I don't know what's going on anymore."

"It's not true," she said. "It can't be. We never even met."

David leaned back and covered his mouth. He looked as if he had just learned of someone's death. He seemed distraught and when he looked back at her again, he looked at her as if she was a stranger in his home.

"David," she said carefully. "It's not true. Since we met, I've spent all my time with you. When would I even have time to have an affair?"

The silence that settled between them then was brutal. It felt to Natalie as if the world had completely stilled, waiting for what might follow.

"Read the email to me," David requested with the clench of his jaw.

Natalie did as he asked, her voice quivering as she did so. Her words did not quake from fear or guilt, though. It was from exhaustion and desperation. She wanted to read it and learn that it said something else entirely.

The words were even worse out loud.

"She says she has evidence," David said. "Why would she say that if she didn't?"

"I don't know," Natalie said. "But she's *wrong*."

"She thinks she has enough to go to the detectives," David said.

He was calm. He had hardly moved in the minutes that had passed, but his eyes were turning red from stress, and she could see he was deep within his own mind as he spoke.

It chilled her to the bone. Was this the moment she'd finally lose him? As often as that concern had crossed her mind, she hated the way it felt now that she was staring it in the face.

"This is insane," David said. "I'm starting to feel like everyone has gone mad."

"*You* feel that way?" Natalie asked. "How do you think this is for me? Last week my biggest problem was finding more work. This week I find myself in the center of a cold case. A missing person linked to me, and each day it gets stranger. I'm not equipped to deal with any of this."

"I told you not to go and see her," he said, bringing up an old argument.

Natalie sighed. "We've moved past that. This is something new entirely."

"She mentioned this when you were there the other day?" David asked.

Natalie nodded. "And it was so outrageous that we laughed about it. Then the topic was dropped."

David rubbed his eyes. "Do you even have any evidence that this woman was married to Alan? Other than her simply telling you about it?"

She thought back to every conversation she'd had with Amanda, and then with Alan. Despite them never meeting, there had been small details shared between them, and Alan had never actually mentioned a wife.

"No," Natalie said. "Now that I think of it, all I have are her words. That had seemed like enough before."

David nodded. "This hasn't seemed right from the start."

She questioned everything then, including her own intelligence. Why had she believed Amanda so boldly, without there being much proof of anything.

"Were there any photographs of the two of them at the house?" David asked.

"No," she answered, feeling entirely deflated. "At least, I didn't see any."

"And she never showed you any of the documents she claims she has, or anything that proves her identity?" he continued.

"No…" Natalie answered quietly.

Every ounce of strength she'd had that morning drained from her then. The determination she'd felt before to pick herself back up washed right out of her.

It was becoming apparent that she truly was as small and simple as she often felt. Her hands were clammy and her breathing rapid.

"David, what is going on?" she asked.

"How should I know?" he snapped. "This was very much *your* thing. I was against it from the beginning. You did it anyway. This is your mess."

"David," she pleaded. "Please, can we move past all that? I want to focus on the latest message from Amanda. I'm confused and it's making me scared."

"Scared?" he asked.

"Of course I'm scared," she said, tears burning at the edges of her eyes. "I'm involved in something here, and in the process, I think I'm losing you."

Her words had fallen out of her without control, and she had in that one sentence, summarized all of her current emotions. His eyes snapped toward her as if he was seeing her for the first time.

"Natalie, what?" he asked softly.

"All we do is fight, and I'm always at the root of it," she said, airing it all out for him. "You would rather pretend to work than to be in the same room as me, and each day I seem to find new ways to disappoint you. I don't want to lose you, David, but I'm horribly afraid that I might."

While it felt good to get it all off her chest, she still felt horrible about it. David glanced back at his office door. Was he going to escape the conversation again?

"What kind of evidence does she have?" he asked.

"W-what?" Natalie asked.

"She says she has evidence of the affair. Do you know what it is or not?" David asked.

Natalie couldn't believe what she was hearing. "Is that really the question you're asking?" she asked. "I don't know what kind of evidence she has!"

David clenched his jaw.

"David, I just told you everything I'm afraid of and you've just brushed past it as if it is nothing," she said. "I'm really struggling here."

"I'm not going to leave you," he snapped. "Is that what you want to hear?"

"I mean, you could make it a little more convincing, I guess," Natalie said.

David frowned. "Nat, if I wanted to leave you, that wouldn't be difficult to do. Surely hearing me say it should be enough."

"What about last night?" she questioned. "In your office. What were you doing?"

David looked at her as if she'd spoken an entirely different language. As if she'd said something so outrageous that he couldn't comprehend it. She held his gaze, desperate for him to talk her through it.

"That email is serious," David said. "Don't you think we should put our attention there? In particular, when she's threatening to get law enforcement involved."

"You don't even believe she's his real wife," Natalie said. "If that's the case, then what is this all about?"

"I don't know, but we'll discover it as this plays out, I'm sure."

As always, his phone rang at an inconvenient time. For the first time, though, David killed the call. Gravity seemed to triple then as it sank in just how concerned he was.

Natalie looked at him in disbelief.

"You let me know if she sends you another email," he said. "I think she's going to demand money."

"Should I respond?" she asked. "What should I do? Do I go to the police myself?"

"And tell them what?" he asked. "We don't know any facts yet."

Natalie swallowed back the lump that had formed in her throat.

"Should I ask her for the evidence?" she asked. "I could pretend to be willing to confess or something. Or perhaps we could have lunch again and I could ask more important questions."

David shook his head. "Absolutely not," he said. "We have no idea how potentially dangerous she could be."

It seemed ridiculous to think of the woman she had met as dangerous. She didn't even pour her own coffee or cut her own fruit. Danger didn't seem like something she would spend her time on.

David's phone rang again, and he pinched his eyes closed.

"I need to take this," he said through a clenched jaw. "I'm sorry. I'll be back."

He didn't answer the call until he had stepped outside the house and out of earshot. Natalie felt as if she would collapse into a small heap.

She turned back to her computer to read the email again, just as another one came through.

```
Natalie,

I've read what you said about the book. Quite frankly,
I'm astonished. Not only did you cheat me out of a
committed marriage, but you intend to put my
heartbreak and struggles into a book.

I would strongly recommend against it.

I will not allow you to embarrass me any further.
Write your book and I'll take you to court. You have
my word.

Amanda
```

Why did Natalie feel so awful when she had done nothing wrong?

She rested her fingertips on the keyboard as she pondered what to do. She clicked back to her manuscript and scrolled to the first page. Then she began to read, and soon enough she was engrossed in the story she had written. It was good, which was a pity.

She closed the document and hovered her cursor over the delete option. The thought of putting the only working book she'd started into digital trash was devastating to her.

Then it occurred to her: she was doing exactly what Amanda asked. She was about to take instruction from a stranger who likely had nothing on her. If Amanda truly was a scam, she had made the wrong presumption about Natalie, and she would learn that it was a mistake.

She thought about the kind of woman she wanted to be and found her courage. With what little power she had reinstated, she decided to reply.

Amanda,

Whatever you claim to have found is false. I never met your husband, and I don't know what you're playing at. You have nothing.

I will write my book, and I will not be bullied by you. If this is some sort of scam, know that you have failed. Now, please leave me alone before you cause any more disruption in my life.

Natalie

She read it a few more times. There was so much more she wanted to say. Names she wanted to call her. However, she opted for short and to-the-point. When she sent the email, it felt good. She stood up for herself and she was proud.

Hopefully, Amanda would realize she could not be scammed or bullied. Even if she didn't, it didn't really matter.

It was another twenty minutes before David came back in the house. His hair was a mess, a clear indicator he'd been scratching his head. He seemed frazzled, as if he was trying to calm himself down.

"Sorry about that," he said sheepishly. "Where were we?"

"Don't worry, I can tell you're stressed," she said. "Do you need to work?"

David nodded. "I'm afraid so. I know it's the worst timing. Please, can we have dinner together tonight and work some of this out?"

Natalie nodded. "I'd like that."

He walked toward his office and paused at the door. "I love you, Nat," he said.

The sensation of butterflies fluttered through her stomach as a small amount of relief washed over her.

"I love you, too," she assured him.

"Please don't doubt my commitment," David continued. "I know times are tough, but you need to trust me."

Natalie sighed. "I know, I'm sorry," she responded. "Just you and me from now on. That seems simpler."

He smiled. "I like that."

CHAPTER NINETEEN

WHEN NATALIE WOKE THE following morning, she felt as if she'd been asleep for days. A headache radiated through her head. She could recall David's arms wrapped around her all night, but couldn't remember when she'd fallen asleep or how she'd gotten to bed.

They'd had dinner and cleared everything up between them. After that, she had little memory of the rest of the night.

"Oh," she said, covering her eyes from the sun.

The curtains were already open, and the room was flooded with light.

"Are you alright?" David's voice soothed her.

"My head," she said. "I have such a headache."

David chuckled. "You drank a fair amount of wine last night."

Natalie propped herself up against the headboard. "What? Am I hungover again? I haven't had a hangover in years before last time."

She kept her eyes closed as she stretched. David's footsteps moved out of the room and toward the kitchen, eventually returning.

"Here," he said, putting a hot cup of coffee into her hands.

She took a sip, trusting her coordination without her eyes to get it to the right place. The first sip was heavenly. It coated her dry mouth and reminded her she was still alive.

"Did I really drink that much?" she asked.

"Yeah," David said. "So did I."

"Then how are you awake and up an about?" she asked.

She opened her eyes a crack and instantly regretted it. The world around her burned her eyes and caused a piercing pain to shoot through her skull. She covered her already closed eyes with her hand.

"Hold on a minute," David said with a chuckle.

He pulled one of the curtains closed and plummeted half of the room into the shade.

"Thank you," she said softly.

Slowly, she opened her eyes and faced the world. She could feel her body had received some rest. The tightness in her muscles had lessened. Her feet no longer hurt. However, her insides felt as if they were rotting, and no amount of coffee could wash the bad taste out of her mouth.

"Don't ever let me drink that much again," she said.

David kneeled on the bed beside her and kissed her on the cheek. "I promise," he said.

Slowly, the events of the previous day came back to her. She recalled their arguments, the emails and the whirlwind of emotions she had felt then. In her bed, with her warm cup of coffee and the gentle nature of David, she no longer felt fear.

She rubbed her eyes, bringing the world back into focus as she sipped back her coffee. Once again, Natalie had no idea what the time was. She wasn't even certain where her phone or watch had been left. Her hair felt dirty, and she could smell the alcohol still on her skin.

"I need a shower," she said. "I smell awful."

It was only then that she noticed the neat pile of clothes at the end of the bed. Beside it, was a small suitcase and David's toiletry bag.

"What's going on?" she asked, suddenly alert.

"What do you mean?" he asked.

She looked at the clothes and the bags, thinking how obvious her question was. "You're packing," she said. "Why?"

David frowned at her. "I told you last night," she said. "My client wants me on set. I think it's stupid, but they're insisting. I have to fly out and stay overnight. I'll be back tomorrow."

"What?" Natalie asked. "No."

"What do you mean, no?" he asked with a laugh.

"No, I don't want you to go," she said. "They never need you on set. Why now of all times?"

He shrugged. "Something about wanting to get the framing and sequences correct," he said. "It seems they're inviting everyone onto the set. I tried to tell them it wasn't necessary, but they insisted."

"Let somebody else do it," she said. "I don't want to be here alone. Not now."

David sat down at the end of the bed and rested his hand on her foot. "It's only for one night."

"There's the entire day today, and then all night, and then all of tomorrow too," she corrected him. "What am I supposed to do during all that time?"

David smiled. "You were writing pretty well yesterday," he said. "You'll have plenty of time to work on your book without interruption. You and Barley can have some quality time together. Doesn't that sound fun?"

She crossed her arms. "No," she answered.

He gave her a knowing look. "I can't have someone else do it," he said. "They're paying me for my time on set and we need the money."

"There's other work," she pleaded. "It just doesn't feel like a good time for you to leave."

He nodded. "I know," he said. "I'm sorry, but I have to do it. I'll call you all along the way, I promise. When I get back, I'll take a day or two off. Sound good?"

Natalie knew there was little she could do to change his mind. "Okay..." she said with a quick nod.

"Good," he said with a slight smirk. "Now, help me choose my shirts for the next two days."

Natalie's shoulders dropped as he reached for the options. Three variations of the same grey shirt. She picked whichever one was in the center and pretended it was her favorite. In reality, it didn't matter, and she didn't care.

He finished packing and zipped up the suitcase, tapping it twice as if to check it was secure.

"What time do you need to leave?" she asked.

"In an hour-and-a-half," he answered. "There's still time for us to have another cup of coffee together."

"What should I do if something happens and you're not here?" she asked. "What if the police show up, or I hear something from Amanda again or something?"

She placed her empty cup down and hugged her knees, resting her heavy head for a moment.

"Nothing is going to happen," he assured her. "I'll admit, I think I overreacted a little yesterday."

"Do you think?" she asked. "I was probably there with you."

David laughed more easily and freely than she'd heard him laugh in some time.

"I've thought about it a little more. I know you didn't have an affair. It's like you said, you were with me all the time in the beginning. There was no chance for you to be fooling around," he said.

"Yeah," she said dramatically with her eyes wide. "Ya think?"

"If she is simply trying to scam you, she will send a demand. We will refuse it and that will likely be the end of it. You never gave her our address, did you?" David asked.

"Of course not," she said. "It's not the sort of thing that comes up in casual conversation."

"Good," he said.

He held out his hand to help her out of bed. They walked together to the kitchen for the cup of coffee he'd promised her. The steam from the coffee swirled against the crisp morning air. She glanced outside and saw dark rain clouds gathering, threatening a wet afternoon.

"You're going to be fine without me," David said. "Maybe a little bored, but that's the worst that could happen?"

She pursed her lips and pretended to sulk. "I don't even remember you telling me about this last night," she said. "Clearly, I went well past my cut-off point. Was I a mess?"

David chuckled. "Not at all. Truthfully, you didn't seem all that drunk. I was surprised to see when we reached the bottom of the second bottle."

"Two bottles?" she asked in shock. "We drank two bottles?"

David smiled. "Yeah, it's like we drank one bottle each."

"And you look as fresh as a daisy," she said, glaring playfully at him. "And I feel as if I've just crawled out of a dumpster."

"Well, I woke up a few hours earlier than you, so I've had a head start on the freshness," David said.

He was like a different person compared to the previous days. Whatever they had spoken about the night before, they had clearly worked it all out. Natalie only wished she could remember what they'd actually said and agreed upon. She was sure it would come back to her eventually.

"Alright, I better get going," he said, dampening her mood.

"Are you sure?" she asked. "You can't stay ten more minutes?"

"I'm already fifteen minutes later than I'm comfortable with," David said, leaning over to kiss her. "I'll call you when I'm at the airport, and I'll call you when I land. Both ways."

"Okay," she said, tugging on his shirt to pull him in for another kiss.

With that, he reached for his small suitcase and left her alone in the house. Everything around her was excruciatingly quiet. There was no conversation, no noise from David's work, and none of his music or incessant sound clips playing.

She sat at the kitchen counter for a moment and waited for inspiration to strike. It did not find her. Eventually, she settled on the sofa and opted to watch a movie. There was, of course, a book to write, but her mind had turned to mush from the wine, and she wasn't feeling brave enough to check her emails again.

Natalie chose a movie with an attractive title, only to discover that it was the kind of movie that would make her cry. So, she rushed to switch it off.

Her eyes caught sight of her computer, and the thought of Amanda's emails trickled into her mind. It rang in her head then that she had no proof that Alan had even disappeared, or that he was her husband to begin with. She wondered if her "private investigator" Charles was her real husband—her partner in crime.

All she had was Amanda's words, and that should never have been good enough to follow so blindly. She reached for the pillow and covered her face. Barley hopped up on the sofa and sniffed her all over.

"Barley," she said, peering over the pillow at him. "I'm not a smart woman. I made a real mess. The kind only a dimwit could make."

How had she been so swept up in all of it without even a shred of evidence? Had she truly lost her mind?

Barley nestled up to her, at ease now that David was out of the house. Natalie accepted the cuddles happily as the first few drops of rain landed against the glass. The sky was dark, and the sun that had tortured her eyes had set.

She jumped when her phone rang.

"David?" she answered. "You gave me a fright."

"I'm just letting you know that I'm at the airport," he said. "It's started to rain."

"Here too," she said. "Glad you made it there safely. Text me when you board and all that, yeah?"

"Of course," he said.

She glanced at the bookshelf and searched through the titles— just in case there was something that caught her fancy. Her head was still throbbing, though, and nothing seemed particularly interesting to her then.

"I love you," she ended the conversation and hung up.

Another cup of coffee might have helped, but then she'd have to move Barley. Natalie simply wasn't ready to do that.

Alone with her dog, things were how they always had been before David, only she had no work to keep herself busy. It was viciously apparent then just how alone she'd been her entire life before he came along.

"You're going to have to get used to him, I'm afraid," she whispered before kissing Barley on the head. "Because I'd really like for him to come back."

Barley stretched and closed his eyes, making himself ready for a long nap. Natalie could do little more than stare out of the window and watch as the water droplets pooled onto the ground below.

By the time David let her know that he'd landed, she still hadn't moved.

CHAPTER TWENTY

THE NEXT DAY, EVERY inch of the house had been cleaned. Facing her book wasn't an option. It made her think of Amanda, which only made her angry.

However, the more she cleaned and scrubbed, the more peace filtered into her mind, pushing out those negative thoughts. And it hadn't stopped at the surfaces and floors. Natalie had tipped all her clothes into a large pile on the bed, more than half of which was sent out in trash bags.

She no longer wanted to be the woman she'd seen in the mirror the last weeks. There needed to be a change. With no distractions, it was the perfect time to instigate one.

Already, she was beginning to feel refreshed. With each swipe of her cloth and toss of a trash bag, it was as if she rid herself of mental baggage. Her goal was to provide David with a better life when he returned.

They were both tired of arguing, and she was the woman with the power to change it. Natalie didn't want to lose him. If there was something she could do to change that possibility, she would.

Of course, David was growing tired. All he did was work, and she had stopped trying to impress him months ago. It made her feel bad to think of it that way, but she was trying to be realistic.

The mess she'd made with Amanda had shown her just how far she had recessed into her own mind. And to top it off, it had potentially put her in danger.

However, there was only so much she could clean in their small home before she was repeating herself. She could think of only one other thing to do. Barley was quickly strapped into his lead, and they headed out for a walk through the neighborhood.

She hadn't realized just how cold it was outside until she had left the house. All her busy work had helped her work up a sweat. That sweat was rapidly cooling against her skin as she headed off in the direction of a nearby park.

Barley walked as if he was in no mood for it. He dragged his feet and stopped every few yards to sniff at something. Normally, Natalie might have tugged at him, urging him to move along. That day, however, she didn't mind the slower pace.

There was nothing else to do, and there was nobody waiting for her when she got home. So, they ambled on.

Natalie brought her headphones with her, and she had the idea of listening to an audiobook while she walked. She recalled that David had gifted her an audiobook before they'd moved, and she'd been too angry with life at the time to listen to it.

She glanced at the cover and noted that it was a self-help book of some sort. She pressed play, eager to have her mind filled with something other than her own thoughts. However, she was quickly reminded just why the audiobook had made her so angry in the first place.

The book was about building confidence and finding one's voice. At the time, she didn't believe it had been a problem in her life. Natalie recalled just how upset it had made her to learn that David felt she needed more confidence.

Now, after some introspection, she understood that he was merely trying to help. From the outside, he'd been able to understand exactly where she was struggling.

So, she listened to the words as the soft, manly voice filtered into her mind. The introduction had been a rundown of the author's credentials, none of which meant anything to Natalie.

What followed, though, felt as if the book had been crafted specifically for her. It was as if she was listening to an infomercial that offered her the single product that could solve all her problems.

The audiobook kept her company on her walk as she and Barley moved slowly along the path. The rain started again, and so Barley picked up the pace, eager to get back home.

By the time they made it to her front door, they were completely soaked. Barley took all of three steps into the house and shook out the dirty water from his fur, sprinkling her clean floors with it.

"That's okay," Natalie whispered. "It gives me something to do later again."

Natalie was soaked to her core as well and headed eagerly for the shower. The water and the steam warmed her up. However, she kept the audiobook playing loudly from her phone. It made her feel less alone in the home as she contemplated what she would do for dinner.

While she would hate to admit it out loud, the book was teaching her something. It was slowly starting to change the way she saw herself and the situation that she was in. Most surprisingly, it was working. The more she listened, the more capable she felt of handling all the things that scared her.

David had been right all along. She had needed it. If only she'd listened to it then, rather than all those months later. Perhaps then, things might have gone differently. Natalie stepped out of the shower and wiped the steam from the mirror.

She stared at her reflection in the mirror and saw the same, boring old face that had been looking back at her for years. It had been about fifteen years since she'd changed anything substantial about her appearance.

Natalie knew what she needed to do.

It took only a few seconds to rush to the garage and return with her kitchen scissors. Using her old brush, she parted the front sections of her hair and combed it down over her face.

She measured once, and then another dozen or so. Finally, she made the first cut. Her nose stuck out through the gap she'd cut in her hair and there was no turning back. So, she continued on, as carefully as she could, until more of her face was exposed from behind her hair.

Finally, she took a step back and considered her work. While it had succeeded in making her seem like a new person, it still needed a lot of work. She kept working at it, cutting fine pieces as she did her best to bring it all together.

It took longer than she'd anticipated—almost forty minutes. Eventually, though, there was nothing more she could do. It was far from perfect, but her new bangs made her feel like a new woman.

She dried her hair and styled it. Then, staring at herself in the mirror, she made a silent promise that she would try harder. It was the least she could do, and her only remaining option. It helped that the voice from her phone was so inspiring and supportive.

Everything that day had made her feel better about herself. She knew then that the worst thing she could do was allow Amanda to bully her. She had a book to write, her financial future potentially depending on it, and Amanda was a lying stranger. Who was *she* to dictate whether or not her book should be written?

Natalie, blinking through her new bangs, sat down at her computer and opened her document. She started writing, creating scenes and characters, filling page after page until she had most of a chapter written out in its barest form.

Then, as if without thought, she opened her portfolio and resume, rewording what no longer aligned with her. The *new* Natalie wouldn't accept defeat. No—she would take her life back.

Once that was done, she looked up specialists in animal behavior. There had to be a way for David and Barley to get along—she had simply not looked hard enough to find it. To her surprise and glee, there were several options to choose from.

That had been enough for now. Natalie padded over to the kitchen and poured herself a glass of white wine with heaps of ice, then returned to her desk.

She leaned back, and by muscle memory, clicked on the email icon. Another message from Amanda waited for her there.

```
You can deny it all you want, but photographs don't
lie.
```

That was all it said. Natalie waited for it to bother her, to dampen her spirits, or for the familiar feeling of stress to overcome her. None of that came. Instead, she heard the words that had been read to her a few hours prior in her audiobook.

The voice had told her that when it came to confrontation, her best chance at survival was to face it head-on, and to get there first. She sipped her wine as she considered what she might do.

Natalie had nothing to hide. She had done nothing wrong.

However, she had not considered just how little she'd eaten that day, and as the wine flowed through her system, her judgment clouded. What felt like confidence was likely rather something closer to arrogance.

In her alcohol-controlled state, she decided that the greatest power move she could adopt was to take her new self to Amanda's house and demand to see the evidence in person. Then, she could rebuke Amanda's words and convince her, rather triumphantly, to leave her alone.

However, she was not going to achieve that in her pajamas. Natalie rushed over to the bedroom and pulled open the doors to her recently repacked wardrobe. There wasn't much left for her to choose from, but she opted for something dark and well-fitted.

Then, she put on the first bit of makeup she'd worn in months and checked her new hairstyle in the mirror one last time.

"This ends now," she said to Barley as if she was on the set of an action movie.

She made sure the dog was fed, and that she was truly ready to face the world. Then, the new Natalie slid into her car and set off on the hour-and-a-half commute back to Amanda's home. If that even was her home.

On her way, she kept the audiobook playing so that her confidence remained where she needed it to be. She hoped also it might provide her with just the right method to use for the confrontation.

When she stopped at the first traffic light, she thought of what happened the last time she'd been on that drive. She reached into her bag for her phone and typed out a text to David.

Amanda will not push me around. This will be dealt
with tonight. I'll let you know how it goes.

She knew he wouldn't approve of her methods, but he wasn't there to stop her. All Natalie had to do was make sure it worked in her favor—then he'd have nothing to argue about.

She checked her reflection in the mirror, making sure her new bangs were still in place, and set her mind to purpose.

CHAPTER TWENTY-ONE

THE LAST TIME NATALIE had pulled into Amanda's driveway, her hands were clammy from nerves and stress. That day, however, Natalie was fired up. She could feel a small layer of sweat on her skin, but it was not from nerves or fear that time. It was from being completely prepared to take back her life.

She came into the driveway so fast she almost had to slam the brakes. Natalie checked her appearance one last time in preparation for her surprise appearance at Amanda's door.

Her heart pounded fiercely in her chest as she approached the front door. In her mind, she was doing her best to figure out what she would say first. And how exactly she would convince Amanda to even enter a conversation with her.

There was always the chance Amanda might not even open the door, as she could see her through the doorbell camera. She knew it was a little too late to be contemplating all those things, but it might not have been too late for a miracle.

Her footsteps matched the rhythm of her beating heart, and soon enough, the large metal door came into view. However, there was a small crack of light that shone through from the inside. The door was partially open.

It was quickly becoming dark outside. Natalie half expected to see someone approach the door or walk past on the inside. However, there seemed to be no movement inside at all.

She reached out to press the doorbell and found it broken. It had been hit so hard that it was hanging out of the wall. So, she resorted to knocking instead, beating her knuckles against the door as hard as she could. The sound echoed through the house, bouncing back in her direction. Natalie listened for any sound of movement from inside.

"Hello?" Natalie called.

Her voice sounded as quiet as a mouse against the large, looming property. Natalie could feel her confidence fading quickly. The cold was setting in, causing the sweat to settle against her skin.

"Amanda?" Natalie called into the house. "We need to talk!"

The longer she stood there, the more unsettled she felt. The quiet that came from inside the house felt loud. There were many lights on, which told her that someone was likely home. But the broken doorbell and open door told her something wasn't right.

She wasn't sure what to do. She reached out and pushed the door and it swung open in front of her. Perhaps with more space, her voice could travel a little further.

"Hello?" she called again, feeling a little foolish at how long she'd already been standing there.

Natalie bit her lip. She didn't even have Amanda's number, otherwise she could have called to let her know she was standing outside. Had her drive there been wasted?

For a moment, she considered getting in her car and turning back, but she couldn't get herself to do it. Something in the depths of her being tugged at her, urging her to stay. So, without knowing what else to do, Natalie stepped inside.

"Amanda?" she called out again.

She paused. It felt as if she had walked into a room where the conversation had fallen silent. There was an overwhelming sensation that she'd interrupted something. And even though she knew what she was doing was wrong, her feet willed her further into the house.

Her footsteps seemed to echo into the large, minimalist spaces around her.

"It's me, Natalie," she said as loudly as she could. "We need to talk about this. I want to sort things out."

There was no feeling more uncomfortable than that of being in a home uninvited. Natalie swallowed hard as she carried on walking. The first, and most logical place to check was the kitchen.

She peered into the kitchen. It wasn't impossible that Amanda was using headphones or something of the like and couldn't hear her. But then, surely there would be some noise from her moving about. Either way, the last thing that Natalie wanted was to startle her. She was technically trespassing.

On the kitchen table, there was a half-finished glass of wine and a plate of dinner that had only a few bites taken out of it. The chair was pushed back slightly, as if she'd just been there a minute ago.

"Amanda?" Natalie asked.

She figured as long as she called out and walked, she wouldn't take Amanda by surprise. She might have been sleeping already, although it was still early.

What were the typical working hours of a scammer?

She glanced up at the cabinet and saw where the wine glasses were stored. Natalie's mouth was dry, and her nerves threatened to get the better of her. So, she reached up for a glass and poured herself a few sips of wine from the bottle that still stood open on the counter.

She closed her eyes and took a deep breath, listening as carefully as she could to any sounds around her. The house was entirely quiet. There were no televisions on, and no music playing.

"Hello?" Natalie called again. This time, she headed out to the next room which was one of many living rooms in the home. The deeper she made it into the home, the less strange she felt about trespassing there.

She moved through the living room and into a dining space. Still, there was no sign of Amanda anywhere.

"Sarah?" she tried.

She stopped and listened.

"I'm not a threat!" she called out. "The door was open. I'm just here to have a talk, that's all."

Her steps slowed the deeper she made it into the house. Eventually, she would find someone there and she'd have to explain herself. Natalie had never done anything like this before. The adrenaline rush it gave her seemed to cloud her judgement as she peered through a door that led to the study.

She didn't hesitate to step inside and approach the desk. The walls were lined with bookshelves, filled with binders of the same gray color. They had business names on them, along with years.

She continued into the room until she made it to the other side of the desk. There, she sat down in the chair and reached for the drawers. None of them were locked, and all of them were stuffed full of papers.

She reached for some of the papers inside. The first drawer held financial statements and contracts. On there, she saw the name Alan Peckin with his signature.

"This really was his home," she said beneath her breath.

This meant Amanda most likely *was* his wife. She sank back in the chair as she paged through it all, taking in some of the details of his businesses and contracts. She glanced up at the shelves and, as Amanda had mentioned, saw nothing labeled with Pathfinder Pages.

Natalie frowned. Everything was matching up to what Amanda had said, except the part about the affair. Why would she have told so much truth, only to lie about the affair?

Natalie allowed her thoughts to roll over in her mind a few times.

There had to be more she could find. So, she reached for the next drawer and pulled out some papers. It didn't take long for her to know exactly what they were.

They were handwritten love letters from Alan to Amanda.

She recognized his style of writing. He wasn't particularly good with words, but it always seemed passionate. She read through one where Alan confessed his undying devotion to her.

Some were beautiful. They'd kept them all so they could be read again and remembered. Natalie placed the letters back in the drawer and shut it. How could a man who loved his wife so much walk out on her like that?

From what Natalie could tell, Amanda wasn't wrong. Alan had been obsessed with her.

She leaned back as she tried to piece it all together. If all of it was true, then how did Amanda get her information about their affair so wrong? It was truly impossible for there to be evidence suggesting it had happened.

On the other end of the desk was a mug of coffee, still half full and ice cold. Clearly, someone had been at that desk that day. She stared at the mug as her mind wandered through all the possibilities.

There were contracts that correlated to all the businesses labeled on the binders. She'd seen them in the top drawer. But where were the copies of the contracts she had signed?

Natalie had signed a new one with each book, and so had he. Everything else was neatly organized, but anything to do with her seemed vacant from the space. That didn't make sense to her.

She got up from the chair and reached for one of the binders. Perhaps he had simply labeled it as something else. Still, why would he?

She opened the first binder and found everything to be in order. The same with the next, and the next after that. Soon, she had gone through a dozen with no sign of Pathfinder Pages.

Then, an unsettling thought crossed her mind. *What if Alan never really went missing?*

Amanda had been clear just how much she loved him. While he'd apparently been distant for some time, she had told Natalie all about how strong their relationship had been. It was possible they were working together.

Natalie never really knew Alan at all. What if his choice of business dealings had changed? What if his entire disappearance had been made up, and they were working together to extort her?

She rolled her eyes. "Extort you for what?" she asked herself. "You have nothing to offer."

The more she learned, the less it made sense. Natalie was beginning to feel defeated again. Her attempts at taking back control were rapidly failing. And now, she was rummaging through someone else's belongings in their home uninvited.

David was right, she should have stayed as far away from that house as possible.

Natalie sighed and prepared to leave. She would go home, crawl into bed, and try to forget that she'd ever even attempted to do something so bold.

She turned toward the door, but something on the desk caught her eye. How had she not spotted that before?

A thick envelope, with freshly penned information on it. It was addressed to the sheriff.

There was no way she was leaving without seeing what was in that envelope. It might be the only solid piece of information in the entire house.

Natalie reached over and picked it up. The contents were thick, and of various sizes. It felt lumpy to the touch. She turned it over, and to her luck, it hadn't been properly sealed yet.

She paused for just a short moment to consider her actions before deciding that she'd already done enough to where she might as well just go ahead and look. She opened the envelope and poured its contents out into the palm of her hand.

What faced her made her blood run cold as ice. Natalie dropped the stack of papers to on the table and took a quick step back as her heart leaped into her throat.

CHAPTER TWENTY-TWO

HER HANDS TREMBLED. NATALIE pulled them back to her as if they'd been burned. On the table, sprawled out from where she'd dropped them, were a series of photographs of her. They had been taken from obscure places, and all in public.

Natalie closed her eyes, wishing she would wake up from the nightmare she'd found herself in. She opened her eyes slowly, horrified she was still in Alan's study, and that the photos of her were still there as if presented specifically for her to see.

She took a timid step forward and lifted two of them from the stack. In the first one her hair had been lighter. Through her rapid breath, she tried to remember just how long ago she'd had her hair that way.

Four years.

It had to be, since she'd been to the hairstylist for that particular look as a treat on her twenty-eighth birthday. It was as if her arms and legs filled with lead as reality set in.

She pushed it aside and let it drop to the ground at her feet. The next photograph was taken outside the library. Natalie had her sunglasses on and a bandage on her wrist. She remembered that day. Barley had tugged on her and sprained her wrist, and she had gone to the library to cheer herself up.

Before David, Natalie had always gone everywhere alone. She stared at the photo in which she wore a shirt she'd thrown away that very morning.

She was not dreaming, and she was not mistaken. Those were photographs of her—and there were many of them. And for reasons she didn't understand, they were at the center of a missing person's case.

She reached for the next photograph. It was taken from across a street. She and Barley were moving toward their favorite walking path. Natalie had a coffee in her hand, and she no longer wore the bandage on her wrist.

Natalie pressed her hand to her head as if to catch her thoughts before they ran away from her. Nothing seemed like the right or reasonable response to what she had just uncovered.

Crying didn't seem appropriate; she was, after all, still trespassing in someone's home. Although, she was fairly certain by that point nobody was home. More photographs of her and Barley were part of the stack.

"How many *are* there?" she whispered, her voice tight from panic.

It felt as if she could not breathe—as if the very air was filled with sharp barbs and every time she tried to fill her lungs with it, they clung to her, threatening to suffocate her. Natalie reached back to lean against the bookshelf behind her.

The bookshelf wasn't going to be enough support. So, she stumbled toward the chair and slumped down in it. Her head rested in her hands as a fit of dizziness overcame her.

The last thing she wanted to do was look up and take in more of the scene around her, but she didn't have a choice. If she had any chance of clearing it up, she had to understand exactly what was going on. A tall task, as it seemed the more she learned, the less it all made sense.

In between the photographs, she found one of her old business cards. Had she met Alan at some point, and simply didn't remember? She wasn't in the habit of leaving her business card in random places.

The next photograph made her the most ill of them all. It was snapped outside her old house. She was in the driveway, getting the groceries out of her car. On the back was a short list of facts gathered about her.

```
Lives alone
Dog named Barley
Monday mornings - Book shop
```

Alan was right. She did go to the bookshop every Monday morning for coffee and to browse any new books on the shelves. Natalie had liked the predictability of her life then, but it seemed it might be her downfall.

She placed the photograph down and tried to gather her thoughts. She reached for her phone and called David. It felt as if it took a lifetime for the ringing to start.

"Please answer," she whispered.

She was greeted with his voicemail message. Natalie closed her eyes and clenched her jaw. She tried to phone him again. Still, there was no answer.

What was she involved in? How did it ever get to that point?

What to do about it certainly wasn't obvious, either. Should she take the photographs with her? Eventually, someone would know there had been a stranger in the house. Or did she let Amanda send the photographs to the detectives and deal with it when they came knocking on her door?

Nothing seemed like a good enough answer to her. What she really wanted to do was toss the images into a bin and burn them from existence. She wanted to go back in time and never respond to Amanda's initial email.

A single tear rolled down her cheek. Natalie's leg hopped from anxiety, and she rapidly became exhausted. Yet, she knew there was still more to discover. Among the photographs were folded pieces of paper.

A lump had formed in her throat again, and this time it threatened to spill out of her and all over the desk and evidence. She concentrated on quelling her stomach as hard as she could.

But her head was spinning, and closing her eyes no longer helped her dizziness. Her eyes flew open as she searched for something to focus on, something that could become her anchor in all the mess around her.

She still needed to see more. Perhaps the folded pieces of paper were the missing Pathfinder Pages documents.

Nervously, she reached for one. She folded it open and saw that whatever it was, it was handwritten. Instantly, she recognized it to be the same handwriting from Alan's letters to Amanda.

These were also letters. However, they were addressed to Natalie.

Dear Natalie,

I find it difficult to choose the right words for this. You see, I am a man who acts on instinct. However, that has often led me into trouble, and so I do my best to manage it well.

When I first saw you, I instinctively wished to know you. I tried to greet you at the coffee counter by the bookstore, but you offered me no more than a weak smile before brushing me off. I can't blame you for that. I am a stranger to you.

But you see, you are not a stranger to me. Over the last weeks, I have found myself entirely engrossed in your life. You have captured me in every sense of the word, and I'm not sure I can be free until we are properly introduced.

I do not mean to scare you with all this. I merely mean to reach out in a way I believe might be preferable to you.

I hope you'll understand. More than that, I hope you'll join me for coffee.

Your captive,
Alan Peckin

She was certain she had to be dreaming then. Her eyes burned with more looming tears as she cast the letter aside. What horrified her most was that there appeared to be more.

What did he attempt to do? Was it part of a book he was working on? If so, why would he have gone about it in that manner?

Natalie pressed her hand to her stomach as she tried to navigate the chaos in her mind. She blinked back the tears that tried so desperately to burn her cheeks and reached for the next letter.

```
Natalie,


I have not yet been brave enough to send you any of
my letters. However, I feel I must explain. I hired
you as my editor, but in truth, I have no interest in
writing books or publishing. None of what we work on
will ever see the light of day, and I'm starting to
develop a lump of guilt within me for making you work
so hard.


You see, I only wanted to get to know you better, and
that was the best way I knew how. My feelings are
complicated, but I know that I must be with you. My
life is complex at the moment, but I can sort it out.


However, the longer that I continue down this path,
the more I fear I am digging myself into a hole I
cannot crawl out of. I know that if we simply meet,
you will understand entirely.


Thinking of you,
Alan


P.S. It was so good to see you today at the library.
You seemed relaxed and well.
```

"No, no, no," she said quietly. "This can't be happening. What the hell is going on?"

She scrambled at the letters, each of them seeming as though they had become more familiar. By the fourth letter he was calling her, "Nat."

She understood then how Amanda would have assumed that they were having an affair. After all, that's how she and Alan had met and been married in the first place. He had waited for her tirelessly at the coffee shop.

It wasn't romantic at all. He had been stalking Amanda, and when she no longer gave him his fix, he had chosen Natalie.

Then, he had disappeared, and she was in the middle of a mess she knew nothing about.

There had to be ten letters stuffed into the envelope along with the photographs. None of his letters had ever reached her, though. There they were, unsent and tucked away somewhere until Amanda uncovered them.

It must have been the same photographs he'd kept in the locked folder on his computer. Natalie reached for his keyboard, her hands hovering over the keys.

"Don't be stupid," she said, pulling her hands away.

It would be password protected, and she stood no chance of guessing. She listened to the completely silent house around her and it sent chills down her spine. She was in a stranger's house, snooping through sensitive case material. Natalie was in way over her head.

She looked at the photographs and the letters in front of her and tried to decipher what it would mean. How would that look in court? What would she say?

She never even knew what Alan Peckin looked like, and yet, he had always been so near to her for all those years. Natalie reached for her phone and dialed David a third time.

"Why do you never answer when I need you?" she whispered.

True to his reputation, the call went unanswered. It was possible he was still on set. Where was he? Perhaps she could fly out to meet him and run away from all she faced.

There were more letters to be read, and more photographs she had not yet looked at. She brushed through them in a glance. Panic rose in her the longer she sat there, too stunned to move, until she was certain she was going to be sick.

CHAPTER TWENTY-THREE

NATALIE GRABBED THE TRASH can just in time to catch the spew as it burst from her mouth. It was as if everything that pent up within her over the last few weeks was pouring from her, burning her throat on its way out.

She tried to breathe, but it threatened to suffocate her. Her hands shook and her legs felt heavy. It was so much worse than a lonely woman being duped into a romance scam. She had been conned into working for a man who already learned everything about her.

All those years she'd worked for Alan, she'd been toying with a stalker and never known it. She'd never even thought about questioning it. Why would she have?

Years' worth of crime documentaries shattered through her mind like a rapid slideshow. When she was finally able to breathe again, she reached for her phone and dialed David's number again.

As she suspected, it went through to voicemail. This time, she spoke. She had to say it out loud—it needed to be pulled from her mind before she could move on and decide what to do.

"David, honey, please you need to call me," she said desperately as tears began to flow freely. "It's about Alan and I'm scared. I don't care about the money. Come home. I need you."

That was all she could muster to explain between sobs and sniffs. He would hear it—she knew he would—and she hoped that he'd rush home to her. Natalie began to gather the photographs of her to stuff them back into the envelope. One of them caught her eye.

It was a photograph of her working at a coffee shop. There was so much detail in the image that she was able to see what was on her screen. She had been working on one of Alan's documents. And the entire time, he had been sitting right behind her, watching her do it.

Natalie had tried so often to have a meeting with him. Particularly after they had done so much work together. Alan always had an excuse, though.

Why? That was the loudest thought in her mind. If he had been so obsessed with her that he followed her around and wrote her secret letters, then why wouldn't he have taken the opportunity to get to know her?

And what might have happened if they did meet? Would she have been in danger?

She needed to get out of there, that was all she could think to do. If she could get as far away from it all and back to the safety of her own home, she might be able to think clearly again.

When she reached for one of the pages, through blurred tear-filled vision, she bumped the coffee cup. It fell over with a loud thud and spilled old, cold coffee everywhere.

"Shit!" She scrambling to gather the pages before they were ruined.

As she did so, she leaned over the desk and her body bumped the computer mouse. The screen lit up, adding light into the room and startling Natalie. Already on edge, she glanced at the screen, hoping to catch a glimpse of the time. She had no idea how long she'd been in that room.

What she saw had her eyes fixated on the screen. For a second time, she reached for the trash can. This time, there was little more than stomach acid that came out of her mouth.

Even with an entirely empty stomach, she kept retching. She needed to look at the screen again to make sure that she'd seen correctly, but she was gripped with fear. It felt as if a hot poker was being pushed through her mind as a migraine blossomed into full force. Natalie could feel her sanity slipping from her as she slowly raised her upper body again and faced what she was terrified to accept.

The screensaver on Alan's screen was an image of his wedding photograph. In it, Amanda stood with a wide smile, a simple white dress, and a large diamond resting on her finger. At her side, with an equally proud smile and a neat grey suit, stood *David.*

Natalie shook her head as tears burned her. She couldn't accept it. It couldn't be true. But there was nobody else it could be. She'd been staring at David's face since they'd met, learning every one of his features and subtleties. She had seen first-hand the smile he wore in the photograph.

A different kind of pain hit her in the stomach then. It was of an emotional source, although the symptoms were agonizingly phys-ical. She dug her nails into her leg, wishing it would help her regain control.

She couldn't move. Natalie was glued to the spot, her eyes stuck on the image. All that time she'd been sleeping next to her greatest threat, and she never even sensed a hint of danger.

She thought of the phone call she'd just made to him. Natalie had relied on the threat himself to be her savior. He was the only person she had in her life, and he was a *lie*. Everything was crashing down around her—her entire life was falling apart in a way she could never recover from.

She recalled the day in the book shop when she and David had met. He had guessed her favorite book, but it had been no guess. Natalie had told him her favorite book when she first applied to work for him—when he was still Alan. A job she had always attributed to luck, since an invitation to apply had merely been waiting in her inbox one day.

Horror set in.

Alan's house—no, David's old house—wrapped around her, suddenly frigid and devastatingly empty. She did not feel hidden away there anymore. Rather, she felt so exposed that it made her feel raw.

Natalie, with trembling hands, used her phone to take a photograph of the screensaver on the computer.

How could Amanda not have known David was Alan? Natalie had not exactly tried to hide her husband from the world. She didn't know she needed to.

Instantly, Natalie understood how that could be possible. David was against sharing their personal life online. He had no social media profiles, and didn't want photographs of himself posted anywhere.

She had always thought it was for security issues. However, she knew then that it was because he didn't want the truth to come out.

She gripped the envelope of photographs he had taken of her and clenched her jaw.

She'd all but told David where she was, which meant that as soon as he listened to the message, he might know what she'd uncovered. The man she assumed she knew better than anyone turned out to be a complete stranger. She had no way of knowing just how dangerous he was or how he might react to his great secret being exposed.

All the times they had argued about Amanda, he had known what she said to be true. When he had read over her shoulder about how Alan and Amanda had met, he was reading his own story. He'd been there, waiting for her at the coffee shop. And he'd argued with Natalie over it. He had even gone so far as to blame *her* for the way he was feeling.

Every argument they'd had was pointless. He'd always had control over everything, and she hadn't even noticed. His control had been disguised as a caring hand—a shoulder to cry on. But slowly, and quietly, he had been taking the reins on her life, and she had happily let him, believing he had the best intentions.

Natalie felt like a trapped animal. Her cage was rapidly getting smaller and the air she breathed was being poisoned, and nobody was coming to help. Something wild was set off within her then.

She took off running through the house toward the front door. The grey, modern lines were nothing more than a blur. Where was Amanda? Why was the house empty with the lights on? She hadn't even finished her dinner. Where did she go, and was she also running?

If she could just find Amanda, then perhaps they could help each other.

Natalie reached her car and hurried to lock herself inside of it.

When she glanced in the rearview mirror, she was met with her own tear-stained face. Her makeup had run down her cheeks, a visual show of the rapidly growing fear within her and her total loss of control.

She had to get her belongings—her clothes and necessities. *Barley.* She had to take Barley and get as far as she possibly could. Her tears flowed freely as she drove back to her home. Thankfully, it should be some time before David—Alan—would return home. Natalie would have enough time to get away, but would need to move quickly.

But... where would she go? Her personal bank account was empty, and the tank of gas in her car was rapidly running low. The streetlights reflected off her wedding ring. That would be her only asset.

Natalie would need a clear plan. She could sell her wedding ring and use that money to get her somewhere to stay. She might need to cover legal fees of some kind, too.

"No," she whispered, shaking her head.

She needed to speak to law enforcement first. Somewhere, there was an open case file with Alan Peckin's name on it, and she had something of value to add. Reality was beginning to set in as she thought about how she might explain it all to the police.

All that time, Alan had been right in front of her. He had comforted her on her dark days. He had watched her spiral into depression he himself had been the cause of. He had shown her support when he knew all of it to be a farce.

CHAPTER TWENTY-FOUR

THE WORLD RAPIDLY PASSED Natalie by as she travelled along the road home. Around her, people went about their daily lives as if nothing sinister was going on. Inside her car, she was fully immersed in the middle of something straight out of a horror film.

Her chest heaved as she practiced slow and purposeful breathing. She couldn't allow herself to cry anymore. Natalie needed to focus on the road. The more she replayed her relationship, the more the pieces seemed to fall into place.

They had been newly married when Alan simply disappeared from her life. How much of their life together had been a complete lie? Was he really a video editor, or was that a lie, too? Was that why he always insisted he had to take his phone calls where she couldn't hear them?

Natalie pushed her new bangs away from her eyes. The strands of hair were getting in her way, and she hated the way it felt against her face.

The last few days replayed in her mind, since her first correspondence with Amanda. The emails that had been deleted from her computer along with all her work repeated in her mind. That had to have been Alan, removing the evidence early on. She thought of the way his moods had been changing since Amanda had first reached out, how seriously he had taken all of it, and how desperately he had tried to turn her away.

His lies were catching up with him, and she had been none the wiser.

All that time, Natalie thought he had been perfect for her, but he had merely crafted himself to be who he thought she'd want. He had been watching her, learning about what she liked and where she liked to go.

On their first date, he had miraculously chosen her favorite restaurant, but there had been nothing miraculous about it at all. Rather, it had been carefully planned out.

On her first birthday with him, he had chosen gifts in all her favorite colors. She had congratulated him on being so attentive. Little did she know just how attentive he had truly been.

How many nights before they met had he stared at her photograph? What had he been thinking all those days he'd followed her around? Had he done the same thing with Amanda before he'd met her in the coffee shop?

The more she thought about all the details, the more her foot pressed down on the accelerator. The outside world quickly became a blur. She had her eyes straight ahead of her, not once glancing down at the speedometer. However, she was aware she'd never driven that fast before.

The closer she was to home, the more a plan formulated in her mind. She would pack Barley and her clothes, and leave. There was no other place she could go but directly to law enforcement.

The envelope with all the evidence was on her passenger seat, waiting to be shown to someone who could help. What would she say? How would she word it in a way that didn't make her seem insane?

Natalie knew it would be embarrassing, because that's how she felt—as if she was the world's greatest fool. Her husband had gaslit her at every step of their relationship, and she'd accepted it as the most wonderful thing that had ever happened to her.

She should have trusted Barley's behavior toward him. Perhaps then, she would have avoided all the chaos and the two of them would still be lonely together in her old home.

There was good reason for her to rush home. She had, without knowing it, let him know she was onto him. The voicemail would give her away and she was certain Alan would be headed back as soon as he heard it.

The irony of it all struck her like a bolt of lightning. Natalie had worked all morning and afternoon to turn a new leaf, to craft herself into a new person so that she could move on. Now, after the sun had set on the day, she couldn't remain her old self if she'd wanted to. The old Natalie was gone, and she had no idea who the new Natalie would be. Would the new Natalie even survive?

That was an *option*, she thought. She approached an offramp that would take her onto a bridge. What if she failed to follow the road? What if she simply let her car soar over the edge? She could escape it all, right now. It would be as if none of it had ever happened, and the world would simply move on without her.

Natalie thought of Barley. Who would take care of him? Alan?

That was never going to happen. So, she forced the thought from her mind and pushed onward toward her home.

With that final logic lingering in her mind, Natalie knew she needed a distraction if she had any hope of getting home safely. She reached for the button to turn on the radio.

The soothing voice of the news reporter was just what she needed. As simple as it was, it was a reminder that there were other people in the world.

Breaking news. Someone had fallen from a hotel window to their death. The presenters went into details about the street that had been marked off and the officers filling the area. Someone had been dispatched to report from the scene, and until they got there, those in the studio were forced to fill the time with their own opinions and speculations.

"The deceased is said to have fallen from their window on the fourteenth floor," the presenter said. "At this point, the scene is being treated as a suicide. We're awaiting further details now."

It was a shocking nod to the dark thought that had crossed Natalie's mind just a few moments earlier. She turned up the volume.

The presenter continued, "And I believe our man Joseph has arrived at the scene."

Joseph's microphone came live, and the sound of sirens and chaos filtered in from the background. Every few seconds, Natalie glanced at the passenger seat to make sure the folder of photographs was still there.

"Thank you," Joseph said. "It's chaos here as officers attempt to contain the area. Those who witnessed the incident are being questioned, while others are being turned away. It certainly has placed a dampener on the night."

"Is there any indication as to the identity of the deceased?" the studio presenter asked.

Natalie leaned forward and opened her eyes as widely as she could so that she could focus on the road in front of her. Off the freeway and closer to home, the sensation of imminent danger creeped into her chest.

"Uh, it would seem that word's gotten out already: the deceased has been confirmed as Amanda Peckin, who checked in only three hours ago—quite possibly with the sole purpose of jumping from the window," Joseph concluded.

Natalie slammed on brakes. Her tires squealed as she swerved off to the side of the road. She came to such a sudden stop that her entire body rocked forward, her seatbelt cutting into her from the force.

"There you have it, folks," the studio presenter said. "Our condolences go out to the family of Amanda Peckin. We will remain on scene for any further updates."

Natalie had reached her tipping point. She slammed the palms of her hands against the steering wheel and let out the loudest scream she could. Anger and pain coursed through her, reverberating throughout the car.

If she was going to get herself to safety, she needed to be sure Alan wouldn't find her. She switched her phone off. There was no way of knowing just how far he'd gone to keep track of her since they'd met.

It seemed as if the web she was caught in had pulled tight, and she could feel the ripples of the spider approaching as she struggled to break free. Amanda hadn't been home. She had been at the hotel, falling to her death.

She needed to phone the police to tell them what she knew. However, she hesitated, too afraid to turn on her phone in case Alan would know where she was.

"We've just received further information," Joseph's voice continued. "It would appear that Amanda Peckin was *not* alone when she checked in. Authorities are looking for a tall man with dark hair. They are urging anyone with information to come forward, or for her companion to turn himself in for questioning."

He was *there.* He'd never been on a flight, just as he'd never been a man named David. Alan was closer than she had thought. Natalie pressed her foot down on the accelerator. All she needed was Barley, then she would go straight to the nearest police station.

CHAPTER TWENTY-FIVE

"I'LL BE BACK SOON, I promise," she said to a confused Barley as she secured him in the back seat.

Already in the car were his bed, leash, bowls, and food. She needed everything she could fit into the car, since she had no plans to return to the house. Once she was certain Barley was safe and comfortable, she kissed him on the head.

Barley nestled in and went back to the sleep she had interrupted when she got home. Natalie headed back inside to finish her packing. Inside, she had the television on the news channel.

Amanda's face was plastered on the screen as she followed the story closely. They had no idea what the identity of the man who'd been with her was, but *Natalie* knew. With all she had learned about him, she knew it was no accident, and no suicide.

Her small suitcase was packed with a few days' worth of clothes and her toiletries. She still had no idea where she would go—there was a good chance she'd be sleeping in her car. So, she bundled up a blanket and pillow to take along with her.

Then, she did a quick sweep through the house, reaching for anything that had some sort of value. Stuff she could pawn until she was able to find a source of income again. She had no idea what was to come, but she had no support and a dog to feed.

As she passed her desk, she spied a photograph of her and David on their wedding day. All she saw was Alan staring back at her. He wore the same smile she'd seen in the photograph with Amanda. Still, it was evidence—proof that she wasn't out of her mind.

She grabbed the image and tossed it into her suitcase. On top, she had the photograph, the envelope she had taken from Amanda's house, and some handwritten notes that she'd pocketed from Alan's study. She hoped that the police could use them for a handwriting analysis.

As she took another look at their wedding photograph, she wondered if they even were married. That seemed unlikely, if he was still legally married to Amanda. He had been in charge of filing the paperwork and had proudly presented her with the marriage certificate. The certificate was likely as fake as him.

She kept glancing up at the news hoping they might have tracked him down. Unlikely as that was, hope was the only thing keeping her sane at that point.

Natalie ran through all the ways the conversation could go between her and the police. They would want proof. She looked at what she had and knew there was a piece missing. She had seen it just the day before when she'd been searching for her headphones. The original contract she'd signed with Pathfinder Pages—it had stuck out from behind some old books. She needed to be quick.

Natalie raced over to the garage and climbed over the boxes until she got to the right one. She tossed books to the ground as she rummaged through the remains of her old life in search of the document.

There it was. Natalie paged through to make sure she had the version with her signature on it. It would be the last bit of evidence she had time to gather.

With Barley in the car and her bag packed, she was ready to head out and take her life back. Escape was within reach.

"It is unclear whether this was a suicide or a murder," the news reporter said as she hurried past. "The body landed on the sidewalk, narrowly missing a pedestrian below."

She listened as they explained Amanda had no living relatives to contact. So, Alan has a thing for lonely women, she thought. She rested her hand on the wall as another strong bout of nausea pulsed through her.

She couldn't ignore the role she had played in Amanda's death. Natalie's choice to become involved in the story had put Alan in a difficult position. If she'd never done that, she might have been enjoying dinner with the man she thought was named David, none the wiser. Amanda would still be alive, lying awake and wondering what had happened to her husband. Natalie swallowed it back, knowing she only had to get through the rest of the day—before she wound up like Amanda.

Chilling words from their meeting filtered into Natalie's mind. Amanda had said she sometimes expected him to come walking through the front door again. Was that what had happened that night? Had her missing husband miraculously come back to her, only to send her falling to her death?

She shook her head and urged herself on.

Natalie closed and zipped her suitcase. With one final glance around her home, she prepared to take her leave.

She heard a car pull into the driveway. Natalie stopped dead in her tracks. That sound was all too familiar—it was David's car. She had taken too long to gather what she needed, and now it was too late.

She heard the thud of the car door closing. Barley barked from his place in the back seat of her car. Natalie ran to the kitchen and pulled open the drawer.

His footsteps approached. Just about every light was on inside the house. There would be no point hiding.

She reached in, her eyes fixated on the direction of the front door, and felt around for her favorite chopping knife. It was all she had to defend herself with, and she wasn't about to go down without a fight.

The front door creaked, and he took a timid step inside. Natalie held her breath.

"Law enforcement officers are still trying to uncover the identity of the man last seen with Amanda Peckin when she checked into the hotel," the news reporter said from the television.

"Nat?" he called out.

She took a step back and bumped into the counter, causing a few glasses to rattle. Her heart seized as her feet felt glued to the ground.

"You leave me alone," she said, brandishing the knife. Natalie had hoped to sound fierce and bold when she said it, but her voice had quivered with fear, weakening her position.

"Nat," he said softly, holding his hands out as if to calm the moment. "What are you doing?"

Natalie reached to her suitcase and opened it with one hand. Her eyes remained on him, and the fingers of her other hand gripped the handle of the knife as tightly as she could. She felt around for the envelope and pulled it out, throwing it across the kitchen island at him.

He reached forward and opened it, tipping the contents out where they had shared many meals together. She watched him page through the images and the letters.

"I see," he said, too calmly for her liking.

There was so much hatred in her when she stared at him then that it burned at the back of her eyes. Her hand holding the knife was steady, but her knees trembled where he couldn't see it.

"You might not understand this right now, but I'm relieved," he said. "I feel as if a huge weight has been lifted from my shoulders now that you know the truth."

He spoke as if there was nothing wrong—as if it was a problem they could simply talk through. Barley still barked from the car, and she wished desperately that she had him with her then.

All that stood between her and this sudden stranger was the kitchen island and the blade of her favorite chopping knife.

"I wanted to tell you," he continued. "There were so many times when the truth was just at the tip of my tongue, but we were happy, and I didn't think it mattered."

"You didn't think *this* mattered?" she asked, her eyes glued to him. "Did you think you could just pretend for a few years and eventually you would have a new life, Alan? What was the plan exactly?"

Something flickered in his eyes. "It's odd to hear you call me by that name," he said.

"That's your name," she responded. "You were never David—David's not real."

His shoulders lowered in defeat. "Nat," he started, taking a step closer.

Natalie swung the knife wildly in front of her. "You stay away from me!" she screamed. "Don't you dare take another step closer!"

"Come on, Nat," he pleaded. "It's still me. I'm the same person, I just used a different name."

"You *stalked* me," she said. "And manipulated me! And gaslit me! All this time we've lived together, you've been a stranger."

Every good feeling they'd once shared had suddenly turned to ice and shattered beneath her skin.

"You watched me send email after email," she continued. "I spiraled at the loss of the work—from *you*. The depression, the fatigue, all of it, and *you* had been the cause. You ran my baths and made me dinners to make me feel better and it was all a lie. It had been you the entire time."

"I might have lied about a few things," he said. "The things that never mattered... but I swear I never lied about my feelings for you. That was only ever the truth."

Natalie shook her head. "How could I believe you?" she asked. "You've been manipulating me from the start. You never guessed my favorite book—I *told* you what it was. You used that information to sweep me off my feet."

"I did," he said casually. "And I'm so glad it worked. Please, you have nothing to fear. I would never hurt you."

"I don't believe you," she said coldly.

CHAPTER TWENTY-SIX

UNEASE OVERPOWERED THE ROOM. Natalie gripped the knife, her palm sweaty from fear. There was no sound louder than that of her beating heart—it seemed to reverberate off the walls of their tiny house.

An urge to survive whatever was coming simmered inside her. She felt as if she was bursting at the seams.

"You're not understanding this right," he said. "Think of all the effort I put in just to get to know you. Surely that will prove how serious I am about you?"

"That's ridiculous," she snapped. "I was a target to you. That is not how you treat people. Not how you get to know them."

"All that time that I was watching you, not once did you speak to anyone," he said. "You would greet those in customer service and move on. I couldn't exactly expect for you to approach me, could I?"

"Don't," she said. "The more you try to explain this, the more I realize just how insane you are."

"You don't mean that," he said softly. "I'm still the same man you met and married."

"*Are* we married?" she asked. "Because as far as I'm concerned, you're still married to Amanda. Or you were, until you killed her."

He turned white and swallowed hard. Alan took another soft step toward her. She stared at him, with so much anger in her she wanted to scream. Her back pressed against the cabinets behind her. There was nowhere else to go.

"How could I be so foolish?" she asked in a whisper. "I was so swept away by you, so infatuated that I turned a blind eye to anything you did."

"Nothing I did was with the intention of hurting you," Alan said.

"How is this not supposed to hurt?" she argued. "In which twisted part of your mind did you think I could ever come out of this unscathed?"

"You're right. I should have told you." Alan made no effort to take the knife from her, or to push back. He looked at her as if she was the one who was mad.

"You had every chance," she said. "Do you think I would have turned you away if I knew you were Alan?"

"Alan was a complicated man. A trapped man. David is free," he said.

She scoffed. "You can't just make up a new person to be as you please!" she said. "You don't care about me. Nobody who cares would."

"Then you've never truly felt desperation," he said.

"I feel it now," she said. "Imagine what I might do out of desperation!"

Natalie was cornered. She would need to go through him to escape.

"Where were you going to go?" he asked.

"That's none of your business," she answered.

Alan knew everything about her. He knew she had nobody to turn to.

"I had to find a way to be with you," he tried to explain.

"Why?" she snapped. "Why me?"

"Look at you," he said.

Natalie felt the words struggle in her throat. All the comparisons that she'd made between herself and Amanda, she knew that it couldn't be so simple. She was dull in comparison and always had been.

"I saw you move so silently through the shelves. You paged through books and looked at the pages as if you had stepped into another world. It was as if everything around you was filled with peace. All I wanted to be part of that. The escape, the peace, the quiet. It was all so beautiful."

"How am I any different from Amanda? You stalked her, too, didn't you? All those days at the coffee shop."

"That's not stalking," he said. "I was just waiting."

"These photographs," she said, motioning to the images on the counter. "There are so many of them. One of them was taken outside of my house. In one of them, I'm doing work for you. How do you explain this away? How could you possibly convince me that I'm safe with you?"

"I've never hurt you," he said. "We've been living alone for some time now. If I was going to hurt you, I would have already."

"*This* hurts!" she snapped. "Why couldn't you just do it the normal way? You could have left your wife and asked to meet me."

He seemed to be annoyed by her line of questioning, as if she was the one being unreasonable. What he said was true, though. If he wanted to hurt her, he could have by now, and there was little she could do to stop it.

Natalie had nothing left to lose. The least she could do was try to get to the bottom of it before they crashed over the tipping point.

"You have to understand," he said. "I didn't think it would go this far. How could I know that you would have been interested in me?"

"Because you made sure I would," she answered. "You knew enough about me to say all the right things. You made it effortless to fall for you—to think you were a person heaven-sent just to change my life for the better."

"I *am* that person," he said. "I only knew what you liked because I cared enough to pay attention."

Natalie shook her head. "You're sick," she said, wishing with every word that she might feel less for him. "There has to be something wrong with you."

It was as if something had broken within him then. He leaned against the counter and his eyes turned downward toward the ground.

"There is. Of course there is. Amanda was not the woman you think," he said. "She was... difficult to be with. Controlling. Really controlling. When I first met her, I thought she was brilliant. After a few years of marriage, that changed."

Natalie wasn't sure what she was supposed to think or feel. She felt as if she had slipped into a dream, a different world in which she didn't belong. How could she possibly feel sympathy for him?

"If I had left her or served her with divorce papers, she would have made my life hell," he explained. "She would have destroyed me. She was ruthless, and I couldn't go through it."

"Really?" Natalie asked. "That's ridiculous and you know it. So you run away from your life and start a new one? That's not how things work."

"I'm sorry, but what were you doing just now?" he pointed out. "And it did work. I walked out and right into you. And I regret none of it."

"You don't see how this is different?" Natalie asked. "This can't just be because you're worried about the divorce settlement. There must be more you're not telling me."

"I'll tell you everything you want to know," he said, slipping into the seat at the kitchen island.

"Pathfinder Pages," she said. "All that work I did—was it for any purpose? I read the letters you wrote. Tell me the truth."

"The books were never published," he said. "I set up the business to access my funds without drawing attention. Amanda controlled our bank accounts. She took everything from me, always. I no longer had a life of my own. I needed a business she didn't know about."

"And it was working, wasn't it?" Natalie asked. "Until she found out about Pathfinder Pages. You realized you were under threat then, didn't you?"

"Yes," he said. "We both were."

"Let me make something perfectly clear," Natalie said, feeling completely thin. "I was under threat the moment you approached me the day we met, I just didn't know it. You talk about Amanda being controlling, well what about you?"

He clenched his jaw as if her words had hurt him. Did a man like that truly ever feel hurt? Did he have any feelings at all?

"Was this so you could feel some sort of power?" she asked. "Was I just someone for you to control?"

"No, Natalie! I love you. I really do. Everything I've done is to protect you."

"From *what?*" she asked. "The only thing I needed to be protected from was you."

"From your sadness, your loneliness. From not sharing your life with anyone. Can't you see? Hasn't your life been better since we met? How can I get you to trust me?" he asked.

She stared at him in disbelief. There was no chance for there to be trust between them again. Natalie struggled to hold the knife up. Every few moments, she would raise it again. It was her only line of defense.

"Are you even a film editor?" she asked.

Alan shook his head. "No. I've never done that in my life. I needed something to tell you about how I made my money. I will admit, that was not my most thoughtful lie."

She nodded. "So, when I found you the other night sleeping on the sofa…"

"That's what I do often," he confessed. "Or I read a book, or watch some movies. I don't need to work. I have enough money to support us for the rest of our lives."

There was nothing she could do to keep the tears from rolling over her cheeks and falling to the floor. There was nothing she knew about him that was true. The only truth she had was the fact that he still looked the same way he did on the day they'd met.

"I'm sorry," he said, looking up at her. "When Amanda reached out, I just panicked. All those arguments—the stuff I said to you—it didn't really matter. I was stressed and freaking out and I didn't know what to do or say about it."

Natalie's chin quivered as she tried not to break out into a full sob. It felt as if all oxygen had been pulled from the room. No matter how hard she tried, she could not take a deep breath.

Panic rapidly rose inside her, and she knew she would soon lose all ability to protect herself.

Through sobs, she begged him. "Please, just leave, and let me go. I don't want to do this anymore. I hate all of it and you're just sitting there as if it can be explained away."

Alan rose, towering over her and stepped carefully in her direction. Her knees were weak and her heartbeat rapid. A few more seconds and she would lose reality and faint. She tightened her grip on the knife and kept it pointed in his direction.

"I can't do that," he said seriously. "I've worked too hard for you. For *us*. I'm not about to throw that all away."

CHAPTER TWENTY-SEVEN

"WHY DID YOU GO back to the house?" Alan asked.

The house. Not *her* house. He was talking about the house he shared with his wife, Amanda. The woman who had dropped fourteen floors to her death not too long ago. He wasn't afraid of her or her knife, and there was little she could do to change that. No matter how often she thought about plunging it into his ribcage, he still looked like the man she'd fallen in love with and married. Until just a few hours before, she had only known him as David—the love of her life.

She searched him for a sign of the man she'd known. She was faced with her husband, by law or not—a man who she had been the most intimate with. The one person she had relied on for everything in her life.

Until that afternoon, she thought she knew everything about him. He knew everything about her, too. She had been happy to show it all to him.

"I listened to the book you bought me," she answered.

He smirked, and she hated him for it. "Finally," he said.

Why did it matter? Why did she feel so small when he looked at her then? He was behaving as if they were just in another one of their arguments. As if she was going to simply take Barley for a walk, followed by their usual make-up dinner and talk.

Natalie swallowed hard. "I was going there to straighten things out, to get ahead of the confrontation," she said. "You were gone, and I wanted to make sure you came back to something better. I…I don't think I was thinking clearly." She wondered why she was explaining herself to him. "That doesn't matter," she quickly continued. "Amanda wasn't answering the door, and it was open, so I went inside."

He tilted his head as he considered her closely. "That seems unlike you," he said.

"Well then, it seems that neither of us knows each other very well," she replied, hoping it would help her regain some sense of an upper hand. "I wanted to see if I could get her attention."

Alan glanced at the envelope on the table. "You got more than that, by the looks of it."

She thought back to the moment when she was walking through Amanda's home, *her husband's* former home, and how she hadn't known just how much danger she was getting herself into. She had been nothing more than a small mouse walking through the lair of a snake.

"How much did you see while you were in there?" he asked.

"Enough," she said. Natalie glanced at the letters on the counter. "You wrote letters to her once, too. How long would it be before you found your next prey after me?"

"How did you know it was me?" he asked. It seemed as though he no longer cared about her feelings and only wanted to know the facts.

"The screensaver on the computer screen," she answered. "It's your wedding photo with Amanda. There's no way that can be a lie."

She wished he would dispute it. Everything in her wanted him to tell her something that would explain it all away, but they were well past that point. Natalie wasn't sure how much more she could take. He scared her, she loved him, and all she wanted to do was run away.

"How did you react?" he asked, his voice low and his eyes unmoving from her face.

He wanted to see it in her eyes, the shock and the fear that she felt. Alan was getting a kick out of it, as if it was the most fun he'd had in years.

"I'd helped myself to some of her wine, which promptly came spilling out of me and into the trashcan," she answered breathlessly.

"Spoken like a true linguist," he said.

Natalie didn't want to speak anymore. The way he looked at her was wrong. She was a spectacle to him, and she couldn't shake the feeling she was only ensnaring herself further in his trap.

Nobody could have been equipped for what she was going through. There was no plan to follow, no steps to take, and no help on the way.

"I tried to phone you back and you didn't answer," he said. "And by the way, I don't just jump from woman to woman. There's nobody else I want but you."

"I switched my phone off." Natalie tried to settle her breathing. "How can I believe a word you're saying, Alan?"

Alan nodded. "I see. You were going to run. And how did you think that was going to end?"

"I don't know… I hate you," she whispered. She wanted to spit at him, but her mouth was dry from fear. He was taunting her, making her feel like an idiot.

"That's not what you said the last time we spoke," he said gently. "Tell me, where were you going to go?"

Her arm finally gave up, and she lowered the knife. It was no use. She couldn't do it. Even if she could, she would at best land one strike before he grabbed her. Natalie wasn't making it out of that situation without a miracle.

"The police," she answered. "I have all the evidence I need to prove what happened. They're already looking for you."

The news playing in the background was a constant reminder of that. It would only be a matter of time before the camera footage from the hotel lobby would be played across the screen again.

"Yes, so I've heard," he said. "Although, they're really just looking for a tall man with dark hair. That could be a lot of people."

"They'll figure it out eventually," she said. "Who knows what she's already sent them? It's entirely possible they're already onto you."

"They're looking for Alan Peckin," he said. "I haven't been him for some time. I'm David Kemp, or have you forgotten? Alan Peckin hasn't been around for a long time."

It almost looked as if he was enjoying the police being after him. There was no hint of nerves or fear. Alan seemed as if he was in complete control, despite his claims about his life with Amanda. His calmness was something that had originally attracted her to him. Now, it made him seem like a psychopath.

"You're a smart man, Alan," she said. "But you're not smarter than the entire world. You'll be caught eventually. You have blood on your hands. You can't run forever. You can choose as many names as you like, but it will catch up to you eventually."

He shrugged as if it didn't matter at all. As if sending a woman fourteen stories to her death was merely another chore on his to-do list. As if he thought living his life on the run was something ordinary—just another experience to have.

Alan stood close to her, as he often did. She could smell the familiar scent of his cologne. Before, she might have leaned into him for a hug, and he would have kissed her on the head. That would have been easy to do then.

She could melt into him and forget all that was going on and, perhaps, for a moment, pretend everything was as it had been when she woke up that morning. It would take only a second. But the energy between them felt stale and cold.

Alan nodded. "Okay," he said.

He turned from her, gathered the photographs and the letters together, and placed them gently into the envelope. Natalie waited for him to reach into his pocket for a lighter to light it on fire to remove the evidence.

Rather, he turned back to her and held it out in her direction. His hand was steady and still.

"Go," he said. "Don't let me stop you. Do what you need to to get through this. I'm not here to hurt you. I was hoping we could talk it through, and you could understand."

She wasn't sure what to do or think. Was he teasing her? Had she missed something? Was it a trick?

After a moment's hesitation, she reached carefully for the envelope. It released easily from his hands, and she had what she needed back in her possession. Alan moved out of her way and motioned for her to head toward the door.

She shuffled past him and waited for him to stop her. Natalie held her breath.

Her feet felt heavy as she took her first steps. One step followed the other, and she was nearer to the door. Barley's barking had turned into panicked whines.

It was as if chains had dropped from her body, and she was inching closer to her freedom. There were so many questions in her mind, but she wouldn't risk stopping to ask them.

"They'll come get me and I'll point them in your direction," he said. "There's nobody else in the world I'd allow to send me to prison for life. But if I go down, I'm taking you with me."

She stopped. It sounded just like him to twist things in that way. Before, she had simply tossed it up to his personality. Now, she recognized the manipulation, and it was twisting her fear into fury.

She had lost so much time and energy believing in her husband David. Natalie had been so proud of him, so happy to have him around, and so grateful for everything he had done for her.

But he was toying with her life, and he seemed so smug about it.

"There's no chance of that," she said. "You have nothing on me."

"I don't need to," he explained. "All I have to do is tell them that you knew all about it and that you helped me push Amanda from that window."

Natalie rolled her eyes. "That's ridiculous. I wasn't at the hotel."

She gripped the envelope so hard that her knuckles were turning white. A familiar sense of lurching pulled through her stomach.

He smiled. "No, but your DNA is all over the house," he said. "Your fingerprints and spit are on the wine glass and your vomit is in the trash can. With the right choice of words, I can convince them rather easily of your involvement."

"If I was involved, why would I go to the police?" she asked.

Alan tapped his finger against the countertop and sighed. "Perhaps you feel guilty about what we did," he said.

"Stop it. *We* didn't do anything," she snapped. "You did every-thing."

"It'll be your word against mine—and the physical evidence."

CHAPTER TWENTY-EIGHT

"YOU'VE RUINED MY LIFE," she said, her eyes misting over again.

There were no more tears left to cry. Her head pounded from the stress and her shoulders had pulled tight. Natalie felt as if she was no longer part of her own body. She was a ghost of the woman she'd been when she woke up that morning.

"You changed your hair," Alan said, as if he hadn't heard her.

He walked to the fridge and retrieved a bottle of white wine. She watched wordlessly as he poured two glasses. Why wasn't she running? That was what she wanted to do, but her feet felt as if they had grown roots, keeping her in place.

"Have you lost your mind? Do you not care about what is happening here?"

He handed her a glass of wine. "I'm assuming you'd like some?" he asked.

She glared at him, refusing to take the glass. He placed it down on the counter closest to her and sat down again. He took a large sip, sighing after to emphasize his enjoyment.

"I like your hair like that," he said. "It's different, but I can easily get used to it."

"Let me make something completely clear," she said. "When I leave here, you will never see me again until we are in court."

"I suppose that's your choice," he said.

"My choice?" she asked in desperation. "What other choice do I have? Do you expect me to just stay? To forgive you?"

"You could, if you want to," he said. "And we can go back to the way things were. Except, of course, now you know the truth about me, you know that we don't have to work so hard. We can go anywhere you'd like—anywhere in the world."

Natalie shook her head. "That's not how this works," she said.

"Why not?" He sipped his wine.

Slowly, she started to feel herself come back. "I have a conscience," she answered. "I can't walk away from this and pretend as if nobody got hurt."

"Are you talking about Amanda?" he asked.

"Of course I'm talking about Amanda!" she shouted as she stepped back toward him. "And I'm talking about me. Does it not occur to you how you've hurt me? I keep telling you about it. Just because you didn't *mean* to, doesn't mean you didn't."

He slumped and rubbed his head. "I really am in no mood to argue with you," he said. "It seems as if that's all we do nowadays."

"Have I lost my mind?" she asked. "Alan, am I crazy? I'm starting to feel as if I am. Do you and I not live in the same reality?"

The glass of wine was beckoning to her. She rushed forward and took it. Alan was not behaving like a threat. She was free to go, and she would. But while she had him, she would use the chance to get everything off her chest.

"I will be leaving here," she said, taking a large sip. "And I will make sure you're sent to prison. Take me down with you if you must, what difference does it make?"

"Of course it makes a difference," he argued. "You'll lose your freedom, your life. That's a big deal."

"What life?" she asked. "You've taken all of it. I have no career or income. There is nobody else in my life. There will be nothing left for me after this, so why shouldn't I just burn with you then?"

"So, we must both suffer because you want to do the right thing?" he asked. "The right thing for who? It's not the right thing for me, and I'll make sure it isn't the right thing for you, either."

"It's the right thing," Natalie said, waving her hand through the air. "You know, what's right? What's fair? The entire reason the world has laws?"

"People break the law all the time," he said.

"Not like this," she snapped. "You're insane."

Alan laughed loudly. "If you say so," he said. "I'm still the man you married, though. You can't be with someone this long and not know them. You just simply know me better now."

Natalie was swigging back the wine, hoping it would help her put an end to their crazy conversation and send her running. Why could she not leave? She knew she should have.

It was him. He had been the love of her life, and that was impossible to simply walk away from. Her minuscule amount of confidence had once again become her greatest enemy.

"You know, I don't feel any different about you," he said. "Even though you're threatening to turn me over to the law. You're talking to me about ending my life and it's made no difference to how much I love you."

It was the first time she'd seen any amount of emotion in him. He cleared his throat and his eyes reddened. Was he going to cry?

"I don't expect you to understand all of this," he said. "And I don't expect you to forgive me, either."

"How could I ever?" she asked. "You've turned my entire life upside down. That's not the behavior of someone who loves me."

"Everyone shows love in a different way," he argued. "I kept you safe and we have a roof over our head… and wine in the fridge. I was there for you all the time. Those things I meant."

"But you're not that person," she said. "That person was David Kemp. In my eyes, David Kemp no longer exists."

"And in mine, Alan Peckin stopped existing years ago. Who do you need me to be?" he asked.

She shook her head. "I don't need anything from you anymore. You can't turn back time and tell me the truth or do the right thing."

"There we have that term again," he said with a chuckle. "The *right thing.*"

She widened her eyes. They were growing heavy from the day's exhaustion.

"Why is that concept so foreign to you?" she questioned. "Normal people understand what the right thing is."

"I could argue that I did the right thing," he said. "Everything I did today was to protect you. Can't you see that?"

"No," she said seriously.

"I got rid of the threat," he explained. "When I saw her accuse you of the affair, I knew she would take everything from us. It was only a matter of time. You don't understand how determined she is. I couldn't sit by and do nothing about it."

"You could have come clean," she said. "You could have told me the truth, and you could have told her the truth, too. That would have been much easier on both of us."

"She's not suffering," he said casually. "Although, she certainly wasn't expecting me to walk through her door today."

It was a chilling thought. She recalled how Amanda had said she sometimes dreamed of that precise scenario. Only, she couldn't have known that it would be her last moments.

"How did you get her to the hotel?" she asked.

"I told her that if she came with me, I'd tell her everything," he said. "And promised her I'd treat her to her favorite room service. Champagne and a fruit platter."

Natalie kept sipping the wine, hoping it would dull her senses since she wasn't sure how much more she could take.

"Would it help if I apologize?" he asked.

She considered reaching forward and slapping him in the face for being so smug about it all.

"What?" she whispered. "No, that wouldn't help. What difference would that make now?"

He shrugged. "Well, I'm sorry anyway. I hate to see you cry, and I hate it even more to be the cause of it. I want you to know this is difficult for me, too."

"Not from where I'm standing," she said. "From here, you look as if this is no big deal. It seemed as if you aren't worried about anything at all."

"How would you prefer I act?" he asked.

Alan got up from his seat again. He kept a close eye on her as he moved around the kitchen counter. She took a step away from him.

"Would you prefer I panic?" he asked. "Would it be helpful if I broke out in a sweat and paced back and forth?"

"Maybe," she said.

"That's not my style," he answered.

Her glass was almost empty. Natalie had gotten all she needed from the conversation. It wasn't what she wanted—she didn't want any of it—but it had been enough. She could say with absolute certainty then that he was a stranger to her.

"Think about this carefully," he said. "I can implicate you in all of this. Even with a plea deal, you're looking at doing a lot of time. Amanda's death was fairly public. Many people were traumatized."

Natalie's mind was slipping. She struggled to think straight. It was as if every ounce of stress she'd been through that day was mounting on her that minute. Physically, she felt as if the air in the room was bearing down on her.

It was heavy, and she struggled to keep her back straight. Natalie needed to leave now. Her strength for what lay ahead was quickly dwindling.

"I'll see you on the other side," she said and immediately wondered why she said something so odd. Natalie emptied her glass and put it down on the kitchen counter. Only, she missed, and the glass fell to the floor and shattered.

"You've been living on my money from Pathfinder Pages," Alan said. "It would be easy to convince a jury that you knew about everything all along. That you twisted my arm into pushing Amanda from that window when she threatened our safety."

"And I'll dispute it all the way," she said.

"Not if we get caught together," he said. "If the police show up here now and see us together, sharing a glass of wine, things might look different."

"Did you set me up?" she asked.

"Have you not been listening?" he argued. "I love you, Nat. I wouldn't set you up like that. I don't *want* you to turn me in, I'm trying to convince you not to."

"By threatening me," she said.

"Yes," he answered plainly. "Like you, I have no other choice. It's not my favorite method."

What did he mean by that? She didn't care anymore. Natalie was desperate to close her eyes and fall into sleep, hopefully waking up to a different life.

She tried to turn to walk toward the door, but she stumbled over her feet. Natalie leaned against the wall to keep herself upright.

"You're alright," Alan said softly.

He put his arms around her. Natalie wanted to fight against him, but her arms were too heavy to move.

The edges of her vision darkened. Natalie blinked rapidly to try and clear her vision. She couldn't focus on anything in front of her. She tried to take another step but couldn't lift her foot high enough to do so.

The wine, she thought. It was no use. With every passing second, she was losing consciousness.

"Let go of me," she mumbled.

"You'll fall if I do," he said. "We've had enough of that today."

With the last blinking moments of consciousness, she felt a brief moment of comfort in his embrace.

CHAPTER TWENTY-NINE

NATALIE FELT THE DAMP forest ground beneath her feet. The cold feeling of it soothed her headache. She took a deep breath and inhaled the scent of the wet trees around her.

It was silent. Nothing had ever seemed so peaceful.

Instinctively, she looked around her for a sign of Barley. She could not hear him sniffing nearby, and there were no paw prints in the mud. The moss around of her was entirely undisturbed.

What was she doing there without him?

She took a careful step forward and listened closely. There were no sounds of birds or bugs around her. No breeze blew through the leaves of the trees. It wasn't like any forest she'd ever been in.

"Barley?" she called ahead of her.

Her own voice echoed back to her.

Something drew her forward. No—it was more like it was pushing her away from where she'd come.

Natalie had no idea how she got there or what she was doing there. She leaned against a tree to keep herself upright. The tree's bark was cold and rough against her skin.

Wherever she was, she had to find her way out of there, and she knew of only one way to do it. She would have to keep walking.

Natalie tried to swallow, but she was too thirsty. Perhaps there was a stream nearby. All the greens around her were vibrant and perfect. Not a single leaf had a mark on it from damage or sickness. This place seemed completely untouched by humans and animals alike.

She let out a loud sigh and it seemed as if her breath traveled out ahead of her, blowing through the trees, creating the first breeze she had seen since she woke up. Her shoulders tightened.

A tremor sounded out through the earth. Slowly, a feeling of dread started to sink in. Then, she heard a crack from somewhere in the trees.

"Barley?" she asked quietly, hoping desperately that her dog would appear from somewhere within the foliage.

Only, everything was quiet and still again. She kept moving. There was an urgency to her movement, and she could find the source of it. All she knew was she had to keep going in the direction she'd been facing.

"David?" she called out, but her voice bounced against the trees, returning to her and traveling no further.

Where were her shoes?

Her hair was wet, too, as if she'd been there for some time and had been rained on. The more she walked, the further the pain spread from her shoulder into the rest of her body. She felt cold.

Natalie wrapped her arms around her body, hoping to trap what little warmth she had left. Then she spotted something that stopped her in her tracks. It was a small stone with a hole through it. She had noted it minutes before when she had started walking.

Natalie reached for her back pocket for her phone. Perhaps she could phone David and find out where he was. Or call for help. At the least, she could photograph the pristine trees around her.

All her pockets were empty. She kept moving.

"Slow and steady," she said quietly to herself. "As long as you keep moving, you're bound to get somewhere." She walked in anticipation of panic setting in. Only, it never arrived.

Natalie kept her head down as she stepped over branches and rocks on her path. Wherever she was, the path hadn't been walked in some time. It was overgrown and unclean.

Still, she could easily spot the route that was laid out. It took a few twists and turns. Looking around her, she could not see through the dense trees. What lay beyond them seemed dark and cold.

Then, she cast her eyes upward. Small dots of blue sky dappled between the treetops. However, the treetops did not move. How was it possible for there to be so little air movement out there?

A large tremor set off again. This time she felt as if she would be knocked off her feet. Natalie reached for a nearby tree to steady herself. When she looked down, she was startled again.

There, at her feet was the same stone with the hole in it. There couldn't be three. That was just impossible. It had to be the same stone. That could mean only one thing.

Natalie bent down to pick it up. In the palm of her hand, the stone seemed larger, and the hole more precise. As if it had been created by someone. A marker left there for someone to find their way. If only it had been more successful, in her case.

Still, if there was one marker, there might be another. She continued on again over the same gnarled tree roots and loose rocks. This time, though, she moved some of the foliage away in the hope of spotting more trail markers. She only found dirt and roots.

Something else bothered her then. The ground seemed empty of any dry or dead leaves. There were trees and plants all around her, and no dead leaves on the ground?

She stopped. Natalie held her hands out in front of her. She didn't recognize them. Instead of her own hands, she saw the hands of her grandmother.

"I'm dreaming," she said.

If that was true, then she needed to wake up.

She looked around her for the best way to do it. Then, for the first time since she'd arrived in that dream, she heard the sound of running water nearby. It came from somewhere within the dark trees.

If she could plunge herself into the water, then she could wake herself up. Another tremor carried through the forest. A short, and mild one. If she was only dreaming, then heading into the unknown could do her no harm.

She stepped off the circular path and into the trees toward the sound of the water. All she could hope was that her unconscious mind would allow her to find it. It was darker than she thought, but still, she could feel her way through.

As she moved further into it, the more she was able see ahead of her. The forest slowly changed. The greens of the leaves turned a grayer color until they were so bland they were hardly green at all.

Her subconscious tugged at her the entire time, willing her to stay asleep. She moved as quickly as she could, but still, her steps felt labored and slow. However, she was making headway.

The sound of the rushing water grew louder. Soon enough, she would stumble upon it and toss herself into the stream.

The more she tried to free herself from the dream, the more uneasy she felt. It was as if her awareness of her state caused her mind to turn against her, to fight her attempts at waking.

She heard another crack behind her and spun around. This time, she was certain what she'd heard was a footstep. Natalie held her breath as she tried to listen for the source.

If Barley had been with her, he would have found her by then. No, someone had been following her the entire time.

"Who's there?" she demanded.

Another crack. This time, it was followed by a bright flash and the sound of a camera shutter. The flash had been so bright that it stunned her. Natalie blinked a few times to get her vision back.

Panic set in and she ran. Branches cut at her shins as she raced toward where she thought the water would be. Around her, multiple flashes and camera shutters carried out. She rose her arms to try and shield herself.

Then, the forest around her kicked off into a cacophony of sounds. Birds took off flying and screeching from the treetops as swarms of bugs flew into the air. They slammed into her head and back as if she were their target. She struggled for air as she ran.

Still, her photograph was being taken. What had once been a cold and dark forest felt as if it was rapidly reaching a boil. Sweat gathered in the small of her back and her hair clung to her cheeks and face.

"Leave me alone!" he screamed.

"I'm doing this for us," David's voice echoed around her.

Then, without warning, there he was. His tall body stood right in front of her, and she slammed into him at full speed. He reached for her as she struggled against him. All of it came flooding back to her. The envelope with photographs, the letter, the glass of wine he had poured for her.

She landed on the ground with a hard thud. Beside her lay a page with a contract written on it. The page was signed with the name Alan Peckin, and beside that was her signature.

Natalie pushed the sheet away from her as she tried to scramble to her feet. But David got to her first. He held her tightly. She stepped to try and get her balance as he pulled her to her feet.

Then, she felt it. The lap of cold water against her toes. She had reached her destination, despite all her mind's tricks to stop her.

If she could just get her body into the water, she knew she would wake up. She scrambled frantically for it.

"Let go," she pleaded with him.

"No," he said sternly. "I can't let you go."

Her head pounded as she slammed her fists into his chest over and over again. Natalie screamed—it traveled through the forest around her, echoing through every empty space.

"I love you," David whispered as tears streamed from her eyes. "You need to wake up."

He tipped them over and they fell. Despite the water having been right at her toes just moments before, she felt as they dropped through the air off the side of a cliff. Natalie closed her eyes tightly, anticipating the impact of whatever awaited them below.

She had no choice but to cling to David. Falling through the air, he was all that she had left.

Just before she hit the bottom, her entire world jolted.

*

Natalie's eyes flew open as the car went over a bump. Barley was pressed against her, his head turned toward Alan, and his ears were back as he growled quietly.

"Barley, get over it," Alan said sternly. "The only reason I'm even taking you with us is because you mean so much to her. Count yourself lucky."

As they passed a streetlamp, the light burned Natalie's eyes. Her heart pounded loudly in her ears. It felt as if she had the worst hangover of her entire life. She wished she was still asleep.

CHAPTER THIRTY

SHE REACHED UP AND touched Barley, who instantly responded to her touch. They were in the backseat of her car. Barley crawled over her and licked her face, happy to see her awake.

Natalie groaned. She knew the feeling that she had then. It was all too familiar. He had drugged her.

"We didn't really drink two whole bottles of wine the other night, did we?" she asked.

Alan turned back toward her. "You're awake!" he said as if he was happy to see her.

She lifted her heavy head so she would be upright. Her clothes were all twisted and odd. Glancing down, she noticed she'd had a change of clothes.

"What am I wearing?" she asked, her confusion escaping her lips.

"Your other clothes smelled of vomit," he said. "Your closet was a bit empty so I just took what would work for now. I packed the rest of your suitcase, so you'll be able to change when we get there."

"Get where?" she asked. "Where are you taking me?"

"I'm not *taking* you anywhere," he said. "You're coming with me. I'd be happy to stop and let you out if you'd like."

She rubbed her head. Natalie was in no condition to think straight. Every thought she had felt labored and intense. Slowly, the events of the day came flooding back to her.

"Take a look out the window," he suggested.

She turned her head just as he sped up. A bright flash carried out through the dark night. A speeding ticket?

"What are you doing?" she mumbled through her brain fog.

"That image will make it look like we're leaving together," he said. "It's for my story. Sometimes the simplest solutions are the best."

She rubbed her head and closed her eyes again.

"Oh no, don't fall asleep again," he said. "You were mumbling and twitching the entire way. Barley was beside himself. It's been a noisy drive. He wouldn't stop growling and barking."

Her mouth was so dry that her lips wanted to stick together.

"How long was I out?" she asked. "How much of whatever that was did you give me?"

"The usual amount," he said. "You've been asleep for about five hours. It should almost be sunrise, which I think will be quite pretty. It's expected to be clear today."

Staring through the window, she tried desperately to make out where they were. She'd never been much of a traveler, so everything looked foreign to her.

"Where's the envelope?" she asked.

He reached over and patted the front seat of the car. Natalie shot her hand around and grabbed it. She pressed it to her chest for safety.

"You still want to turn me in?" he asked.

She nodded. "More than ever."

Alan glanced at her in his rearview mirror and smirked. "Well, I've had a five-hour head start," he said. "I gave them our old address as an anonymous tip about an hour ago. I had to stop for gas, so I used a payphone. Before we left, I made sure to leave your emails open for them to find. You know, that last one you sent her is great. It's the perfect amount of motive balanced with threat."

"What?" she asked, her mind struggling to piece it together.

"If I go down, you go down—remember?" he said with a laugh. "Are you hungry?"

"Thirsty," she offered.

"Oh, of course," he said. "Here."

He handed her a large cup of soda and she sipped at it eagerly. Barley licked at the condensation on the outside of the cup. He was heavy on her lap, but he would not budge from his position.

"You've destroyed me," she said softly.

"No," he answered. "I'm helping you. I know we can be good together. You and I have a connection unlike anything I've ever known before."

The more he spoke, the more he sounded like a mad man. He seemed fired-up, as if something exciting was happening.

"I don't even know you," she said. "I never really did."

He glanced back at her, causing the car to swerve a little. Natalie held onto Barley for stability.

"Enough of that. I'm the guy you've always known, Nat," he said. "I promise you. Once we move past this, it will be just like things always were between us."

"You can't possibly think I'm going to *move past* this," she said.

"Just you wait until you see where I'm taking you," he said with a wide, flashy smile. "You're going to love it. Seriously, you should eat something. I'm worried about you."

He handed her a paper bag with a burger and fries in it. Her stomach grumbled. Natalie couldn't remember the last time she'd actually eaten something. She picked carefully at the fries.

"You haven't drugged this, have you?" she asked.

"Nope," he answered. "I have no need to."

Natalie leaned her head back. "Please don't ever do that again. Or, if you do, at least make sure it's a strong enough dose to kill me."

"Don't say that, Nat," he said seriously. "I couldn't go on without you. I mean that."

She rolled her eyes, and it sent another searing pain through her head. Barley whined, noticing the pained expression on her face.

"What exactly is your plan here, Alan?" she asked.

He tapped the steering wheel. "Please don't call me by that name," he said. "I have not been that man for a very long time. As far as the world is concerned, he is gone."

She clenched her jaw. "What would you prefer I call you then? David?"

He shrugged it off. "That's how you know me. Of course, that will have to change again."

She leaned forward, using her hand to stabilize herself against the seat in front of her. "What's that supposed to mean?" she asked. "Are-are you kidnapping me?"

"Of course not," he answered. "As I said. You're free to go. I just wouldn't recommend it."

She had a lot to think about, and none of it was going to be easy. "What do you mean your name will change?" she asked.

Again, he glanced behind him in her direction. "I've disappeared once before, Nat. It was easy, all things considered. And it will be just as easy to do it again. If you have money and you know the right people, anything is possible."

"I suppose you want me to come with you?" she asked. "And just forget all of this forever?"

"Of course!"

"Why?" she pressed. "Why not just abandon me and disappear like you did with Amanda? Or why not throw me from a building, too, since that's your method of dealing with things."

"Because I love you, Nat," he said. "I really do mean it when I say it. I'm not just trying to convince you of anything. I don't want to live my life without you anymore. Just the thought of it makes me feel horrible."

"I don't know what to do," she said. "I should never have had to face any of this. All I ever should have gotten from a husband was love and companionship and support."

"I can give you those things," he urged. "This new life can be whatever you want it to be."

"You already had your chance," she snapped.

"Look, I've already gotten you so deep into this mess. You really don't have much to lose. Come with me, and we give our life a second chance. If you turn yourself in, they're bound to charge you with something. If we get caught, you'll go to prison anyway." He looked at her in the rearview mirror. "This is your only chance at a normal life."

"It will be a *pretend* normal life," she argued.

"Only for the first while," he said. "Eventually, it will become real, and you'll settle into your new home and life. I already have the perfect name for you."

"And what might that be?" she asked.

He beamed with pride. "Grace."

Barley finally settled. He lowered his head and closed his eyes, sinking into a deep sleep. She kissed his head, thanking him for all he'd done to protect her that day.

"Grace?" she asked.

He nodded. "Like in that book I gave you to read," he said. "*Grace and the Wolf.*"

She thought of the book and how eager he was for her to read it. Realization shattered through her like ice, freezing her to her core. She had been Grace all along. He had always been the wolf. Finally, she understood the book, and the reason he loved it so much. It didn't need a conclusion, because there couldn't be one. For as long as Grace existed in those woods, the wolf would be there, too.

Natalie sank into her seat and held Barley close to her. It didn't matter what she chose, her life would never be the same again. Neither option seemed like the easy choice to her, either. So, it would boil down to which one seemed the most comfortable.

"It can't be that simple," she said.

"You don't need to worry about this," he assured her. "I will do it all. You won't have to lift a finger."

Since they'd met, she had allowed him to make the choices and lead her. Why should that dynamic change now?

*

Grace sipped her coffee as she waited for the bill to arrive at her table. Despite being indoors, the bright sun still burned against her skin. She stretched her neck from side-to-side as she watched the world pass her by.

It had become an integral part of her writing process. She needed to get out and watch people. There was no greater source of inspiration. Once in a while, she would reach for her phone and sneak a photograph of them.

Before heading back home, she read through the start of her chapter again. While the book was almost finished, the first few lines of chapter one had seen many versions. This version, though, she was certain was their final form.

Her husband was right. As the weeks passed, everything started to feel normal again. They no longer spoke about what happened.

Barley was restless at her feet, urging her to hurry up so that they could enjoy their walk home again.

"I'm getting there," she said. "Unless of course, I need to rewrite it again. Then we might be here a little longer."

Barley let out a sigh and lay down on the floor again. Grace's foot swung in time with the music filtering evenly throughout the coffee shop. She loved Mexico.

There was much to explore, and the people were friendly. Most importantly, the weather was pleasant. They had settled in a large home with a decent-sized property where Grace had taken up gardening. It had been the only task that could keep her sane when they'd first arrived there.

She adjusted the screen of her laptop to reduce the glare. She swallowed the final sip of her coffee and read her latest work.

Maria and the Devil
Grace Hunt

Maria fell in love with the devil, only he was disguised as her loving husband. A man so handsome she could not see his flaws. A demon so good at his disguises that he had the world fooled—until one day, the mask slipped. They had one big thing in common: they were each other's downfall.

It was good enough for now. She closed her laptop and took up Barley's lead. His tail wagged eagerly as she placed money on the table and headed for the door.

THANK YOU

Thank you so much for reading my book. I hope you enjoyed reading it at least as much as I enjoyed writing it.

I have a quick favor to ask of you. If you've got a spare moment, would you mind writing a review? I'd be thrilled to hear your thoughts on my story. You can leave one where you purchased the book, or at my publisher's website below.

https://hylosis.pub

ABOUT THE AUTHOR

https://hylosis.pub/pages/author-kat-goss

With a passion for exploring strange ideas and reimagining normal situations through an alternative lens, Kat Goss crafts stories that challenge perceptions and keep readers involved. Away from her screen, Kat enjoys unraveling the complexities of human nature and searching for the unusual in the usual.

Kat lives in Stanford, a heritage village in South Africa where she lives a quiet life with her wife and a small menagerie of animals. When she isn't writing, she spends her time traveling and cooking.

ALSO BY THE AUTHOR

https://www.amazon.com/dp/0639789994

Lilith doesn't want to live anymore. After centuries of heartache and loneliness, she is ready to let go.

Her plans are changed when everything she has tried to avoid for decades stops her in her tracks. The decision to attempt happiness one more time causes a chain reaction of events that she could never see coming. She is about to learn the hard way that nowhere is safe. No matter how far she runs.

With something to fight for, and a wavering will to live, she must face a decision she never thought she'd consider. Will she find happiness? Does she deserve it?

ABOUT THE PUBLISHER

https://hylosis.pub/pages/publishing

Hylosis Publishing is an independent publisher located in Chandler, Arizona. We firmly believe everyone has a story to tell or a unique perspective to share. We're always on the lookout for talented thinkers and storytellers.

Interested in getting published? Apply using the link above.